PENGUIN  CLASSICS

BEOWULF

ADVISORY EDITOR: BETTY RADICE

The manuscript of the Old English *Beowulf* dates from about the year 1000; the poem is thought to have reached literary formulation two centuries earlier, in Mercia or Northumbria. The actual composition of the epic is a process belonging to the centuries between the Age of Migration – in which the action of *Beowulf* is set – and the Anglian civilization of the Age of Bede, who died in 735.

MICHAEL ALEXANDER is Berry Professor of English Literature at the University of St Andrews. His book of translations, *The Earliest English Poems*, appeared in Penguin Classics in 1966. Other publications include *Old Riddles from the Exeter Book* and *A History of Old English Literature*, as well as *The Poetic Achievement of Ezra Pound* and *Twelve Poems*. He is joint editor of the Macmillan Anthologies and is Associate Editor of *Agenda*.

This translation of *Beowulf* has been broadcast by the BBC and the Australian Broadcasting Commission.

BEOWULF

A VERSE TRANSLATION BY
MICHAEL ALEXANDER

PENGUIN BOOKS

PENGUIN BOOKS

Published by the Penguin Group
Penguin Books Ltd, 27 Wrights Lane, London W8 5TZ, England
Penguin Books USA Inc., 375 Hudson Street, New York, New York 10014, USA
Penguin Books Australia Ltd, Ringwood, Victoria, Australia
Penguin Books Canada Ltd, 10 Alcorn Avenue, Toronto, Ontario, Canada M4V 3B2
Penguin Books (NZ) Ltd, 182–190 Wairau Road, Auckland 10, New Zealand

Penguin Books Ltd, Registered Offices: Harmondsworth, Middlesex, England

This translation first published 1973
23 25 27 29 30 28 26 24 22

Copyright © Michael Alexander, 1973
All rights reserved

Printed in England by Clays Ltd, St Ives plc
Set in Monotype Bembo

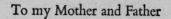

To my Mother and Father

CONTENTS

Acknowledgements
8

Introduction
9

BEOWULF
51

The Fight at Finnsburgh
153

Bibliography
157

Notes
159

Map: the Geography of Beowulf
170

Family Trees
171

Index of Proper Names
173

ACKNOWLEDGEMENTS

It is a pleasure to be able to record my gratitude to Mrs Betty Radice of Penguin Classics for inviting me to undertake a verse translation of *Beowulf* and for her encouragement and editorial discretion. My indebtedness to the scholars who have made the poem available to me is given only token acknowledgement in the Bibliography; I certainly owe much to translations and interpretations which are not mentioned there. It is easier to acknowledge one's pleasant obligation to friends and colleagues who have read parts of the translation and introduction. I am very grateful to Arthur Cooper for his generous interest, his advice, and the example of his own translations from the Chinese. Of the others, I would particularly like to thank Eileen McCall, Felicity Riddy, David Buchan, William Cookson, Roger Fowler, Martin Gray, Norman MacCaig, Alasdair Macrae and Robert Woodings.

A grant of a thousand dollars from the scheme run for the Ford Foundation by the National Translation Centre of Austin, Texas, enabled me to take time off from my publishing job and pass my mornings in the British Museum Reading Room for an agreeable few months in the spring of 1968.

M.J.A.

Stirling, 1 April 1972

INTRODUCTION

'In a place far from libraries I have often read *Beowulf* for pleasure'[1]

THE Old English *Beowulf* has several claims on the attention of modern readers: it is a poem of barbaric splendour and artistry; an eloquent celebration of a heroic life and death; an 'action' of epic sweep and scope. This translation of *Beowulf* began as an attempt to catch in modern English some of that sense of masterful power communicated by the verses of the original Old English poem. As the attempt to imitate the local triumphs of verse and syntax was prolonged, something of the deeper pattern and the real substance and significance of *Beowulf* began to reveal itself. This introduction is an attempt to suggest something of the character of this famous but not very well-known work.

Many people who are not Anglo-Saxon scholars have attempted to translate *Beowulf*, despite its difficulties and its unfamiliarity, and I imagine that they were first of all attracted, as I was, by its sustained energy as poetry: it is an utterance of power. Much of this characteristic power and beauty comes from what I take to be the traditional poetic and narrative forms of public oral performance. Like the 'winged words' of Homer, *Beowulf* was composed to be projected in public performance – to be sung or spoken aloud. It is written after the unmistakable style of oral poetry, a highly-developed medium evolved in and for oral composition and performance, which here can be seen in the first stage of its long adaptation to writing. *Beowulf* is the first large poem in English to survive this transplanting from an oral to a literary mode: it is the beginning of English literature.

9

It is also the end of the epic verse traditions of what might be called English pre-literature. *Beowulf*, then, is a gate into the pre-literate (and pre-Christian) past, through which we cannot go, though we can see a good deal. It is from this Janus-like status as an epic both oral and literary that the powerful and unique character of the poem arises.

Whatever its genesis may have been, *Beowulf*, as I have suggested, is a very considerable poem, and it can stand on its own merits without benefit of introduction by a translator. Its splendid isolation at the beginning of our literature has, however, proved something of a mixed blessing so far as its reputation is concerned. It happens that *Beowulf* is the only long heroic poem to survive complete in Old English. It is therefore a document of prime philological, cultural and historical – as well as literary – interest, and is eminently 'worth studying'. For a variety of pedagogical reasons *Beowulf* was mounted as a sort of a dinosaur in the entrance hall of English Literature. Until recently those who wished to study English at university were only allowed to proceed after a minute examination of the epidermis of this sacred monster – or rather of its front end, for the last third of the poem was rarely used as a translation exercise. In most of those who entered into the promised land of modern literature there survived a belated curiosity about the beast whose latter end they had never properly seen. But too often this interest withered away into a ritual academic joke at the expense of Grendel's mother. Some of the mud that was so zealously slung at the old 'crib and gobbet' approach seems to have stuck, very unfairly, to the image of the unoffending poem.

Such an approach to *Beowulf* neglected what I have tried to convey in my translation – that it is composed in epic verse. The emphasis of this introductory essay is upon *Beowulf* as a poem – as an epic poem. Specific aspects of the poem are also addressed – briefly – in the notes; but any serious student of its formidable minor complexities will, of course, seek help from the scholarly commentators on this much-edited work.

First, the few ascertainable facts about the poem and how it has come down to us. *Beowulf* survives in only one version, in a manuscript now in the British Museum. This copy was probably made by scribes of about the year 1000, and the language is the 'classical' late West-Saxon of the Wessex of Ethelred and Aelfric. The poem, first called *Beowulf* in 1805, was first printed in 1815. Like other Anglo-Saxon poems *Beowulf* is written out as continuous prose divided into numbered sections. It runs to 3,182 verses, which form one-tenth of the surviving Anglo-Saxon poetic corpus and make it the longest Old English poem. *Beowulf* probably first assumed its present shape in the eighth century, not in Wessex but north of the Thames in Mercia or Northumbria, since the traditional composite language in which it lives seems to be more Anglian than Saxon. *Beowulf*'s literary composition is traditionally placed in the Northumbria of the age of Bede, who died in 735, though recently the less well documented Mercia of King Offa, who reigned from 757 to 796, has found its supporters. The poem itself is set in the southern Scandinavia of the fifth and sixth centuries, and contains no reference to the British Isles or to New Testament Christianity. However, as a finished literary work it is almost universally held to be the product of a relatively sophisticated and Christian Anglian court – though one that had evidently not yet repudiated its ancestral links with the Germanic peoples across the North Sea. (The Viking sack of Lindisfarne in 793 would cause the English to think differently of their un-Christian cousins.) As it is, *Beowulf* is taken from the communal word-hoard of the northern Germanic peoples, and it is obvious that, among the Anglian settlers, the story of the poem, and the tales involved with it, must have circulated and developed orally for a long time before they were sorted out and set into their present arrangement and could receive their present focus and ultimate literary form.

The main story of *Beowulf* is a simple one. It is the story of the youth and age of a hero. In youth Beowulf achieves glory in a foreign land by fighting and killing first the monster Grendel in King Hrothgar's hall and then Grendel's mother in an underwater cave. In age, having ruled his country well for fifty years, Beowulf goes singlehanded to fight a dragon who is destroying his people. At the end of the fight both Beowulf and the dragon are dead, and the poem ends with his funeral and a prophecy of disaster for his people, the Geats. This heroic legend is entangled with a set, or several sets, of tales we find in other, later, Germanic histories, sagas and poems. For example, the death of Beowulf's lord, Hygelac, in a raid on the Franks is recorded as occurring in about the year 521 in Bishop Gregory of Tours' *Historia Francorum*, written only a generation later than the event. Other kings and tribes of the poem are likewise known to history, though Beowulf himself does not appear elsewhere. The tale of his exploits against Grendel and Grendel's mother, ultimately drawn from folklore, is related, under a different form, of Grettir the Strong, the eleventh-century Icelandic outlaw. In various ways, Germanic history or legend of the heroic Age of Migration illuminate and make meaningful almost every incident and name in *Beowulf* – and there are many of them. The network of stories around the three central encounters lends the life of the monster-slaying hero a much wider and more complicated significance. The richness and importance of these references are also responsible for the poem's initial difficulties of allusion and structure.

It cannot be denied that *Beowulf* is in many ways a difficult poem, and would have remained an inaccessible one without the concentrated elucidatory efforts of generations of scholars.

Its language and its allusions seem more unfamiliar than those of its French eleventh-century counterpart, the *Song of Roland*, and possibly more unfamiliar than the language and world of reference of Homer in the eighth century B.C. The Norman Conquest and the profound changes in Western European attitudes that began in the twelfth century robbed Old English literature of its posterity. Whatever the reason, the world to which *Beowulf* refers will at first seem strange, archaic and 'unclassical' to modern English readers. It is no accident that the first translation of the poem was not into English but Danish (Gruntvig's *Bjowulfs Drape* in 1820). Despite the efforts of William Morris (who translated the poem in 1895) and the Chadwicks, it is still the scholar and not the imaginative writer who shows us round the world of northern history and legend. J. R. R. Tolkien is the exception that proves the rule. His 1936 British Academy lecture '*Beowulf:* the Monsters and the Critics' has cast a spell over most subsequent critics of the poem. But the common reader, however full of Keats's 'negative capability', may at first find the names of the heroes as strange as their troll-slaying activities. And then, the grafting of Christian comment onto this unfamiliar world of noble wrestlers can at times produce a bizarre effect. 'In *Beowulf*,' as W. P. Ker remarked, 'the hero and the dragon, under the influence of literary convention, pass together from "this transitory life".'

It is prudent to give the devil of prejudice his due. But *Beowulf* really needs no apology; it rises easily above its apparatus. The dying speech of Beowulf to his young helper Wiglaf has the authentic epic amplitude:

> 'Bid men of battle build me a tomb
> fair after fire, on the foreland by the sea
> that shall stand as a reminder of me to my people,
> towering high above Hronesness
> so that ocean travellers shall afterwards name it

> Beowulf's barrow, bending in the distance
> their masted ships through the mists upon the sea.'
>
> (ll. 2802–8)

Like the barrow, the poem *Beowulf* is a monument to the hero,
a massive, elaborate and conspicuous monument containing
gold. As the twelve Geat warriors ride round the barrow, they
utter the death-lament for the hero: it is the ground bass of
the poem.

> Then the warriors rode around the barrow,
> twelve of them in all, athelings' sons.
> They recited a dirge to declare their grief,
> spoke of the man, mourned their King.
> They praised his manhood and the prowess of his hands,
> they raised his name; it is right a man
> should be lavish in honouring his lord and friend,
> should love him in his heart when the leading-forth
> from the house of flesh befalls him at last.
>
> This was the manner of the mourning of the men of the Geats,
> sharers in the feast, the fall of their lord:
> they said that he was of all the world's kings
> the gentlest of men, and the most gracious,
> the kindest to his people, the keenest for fame.
>
> (ll. 3069–182)

They said that he was *lof-geornost*, 'the most eager for praise'
... This desire for 'a name that shall never die beneath the
heavens', for a personal immortality, is the motive that drives
a hero. When he is at the mercy of Grendel's mother or of
the Dragon, Beowulf thinks of his glory; he is *mærtha
gemyndig*, 'mindful of his glorious deeds' – Homer's *klea
andrōn*, 'the glorious deeds of men'. This is the primary theme
of all heroic poetry: the prowess, strength and courage of the
single male, undismayed and undefeated in the face of all
adversaries and in all adventures. The hero surpasses other

men, and his *aristeia* is rewarded by fame. He represents the ultimate of human achievement in a heroic age, and embodies its ideal. Though he must die, his glory lives on.

Beowulf is a heroic poem in the simple sense that it celebrates the actions of its protagonist. Beowulf, son of Edgetheow, is the very type of a hero in that it is his eagerness to seek out and meet every challenge alone and unarmed that makes him glorious in life and brings him to his tragic death. He also has a hero's delight in his own prowess and a hero's magnanimity to lesser men.

Beowulf is a typical heroic poem not only in its central figure but also in its world and in its values. The warriors are either feasting or fighting, they are devoted to glee in hall or glory in the field, and their possessions are gold cups or gold armour, the outward and visible signs of that glee and glory. The society of *Beowulf* is such as Hesiod describes in his account of the age of the heroes, which intervened between the bronze and iron ages:

> A godlike race of heroes, who are called
> The demi-gods – the race before our own.
> Foul wars and dreadful battles ruined some;
> Some sought the flocks of Oedipus, and died
> In Cadmus' land, at seven-gated Thebes;
> And some, who crossed the open sea in ships,
> For fair-haired Helen's sake, were killed at Troy.
> These men were covered up in death, but Zeus
> The son of Kronos gave the others life
> And homes apart from mortals, at Earth's edge.
> And there they live a carefree life, beside
> The whirling Ocean, on the Blessed Isles.[2]

Heroic society is simple: a lord in peace and war is the 'shepherd of his people', *folces hyrde* (Homer's *poimeen laōn*). He gives them shelter, food and drink in his hall; he is their 'ring-giver' and 'gold-friend' in peace and their 'shield' and 'helmet' in war. The warriors 'earn their mead' and their armour by their courage and loyalty in war. Ideally, there is complete solidarity between a king and his people (*folc*).

Hero-tales or heroic poems do not usually remain at the level of simple adventure stories. Even in later medieval romances or in Westerns the heroic code is usually complicated and its values tested by a clash of loyalties: most of the northern heroic tales involve a conflict between the absolute obligation to revenge a slain kinsman or lord and other obligations such as are contracted by being someone's host or guest, or by taking oaths of fealty, of alliance or of marriage. Most of these themes are raised in *Beowulf*, but usually in the inter-related set of stories which support the simple central action; these stories are alluded to rather than related fully. There is a marked contrast between the fullness of epic narration in the central action and the laconic ellipses in which the poem alludes to other well-known tales from the cousinhood of northern story.

This cluster of outside episodes sets the story of Beowulf's life in a much larger context. The development of the foreground story is slow and simple; the episodes are arranged around and behind it, and lend a depth and complexity to the whole. In the simplest of them Beowulf is compared to Sigemund, the greatest of dragon-slayers, and contrasted favourably with the violent Heremod. In the most complicated of them we learn of the series of conflicts between Beowulf's people, the Geats, and the Swedes. These Swedish wars are expressed in terms of a blood feud between the two royal houses over three generations. The blood feuds between the Danes and the Heathobards, and again between the Danes and the Frisians, make two more episodes: both are stories of how a marriage-alliance fails to heal an ancient hatred. Two other episodes deal with murder within the kindred: one tells of an accidental fratricide; the other foreshadows the deliberate treachery of Hrothgar's nephew Hrothulf. Most of these episodes, or 'digressions' as they used to be called, occur in the second half of the poem when Beowulf is back at home in Geatland, and they form a condensed history of the Geat royal house, the Scylfing dynasty. A crucial event in this history is the death of Beowulf's lord Hygelac in a Viking raid upon the northernmost tribes of the Merovingian empire. A messenger at the end of the poem foretells that the Merovingian Franks and the Swedes will descend upon the Geats now that Beowulf is dead. It can be seen, even from this brief summary of the principal episodes of *Beowulf*, that vengeance, the law of the feud, governs most of the stories behind the central action, and that murder can often be heard breathing heavily in the wings.

The foreground story itself is scarcely a serene one. Beowulf's life, though full of away wins, ends in a home defeat. We have been prepared for this by the age of the hero as he approaches his last fight, by the funeral of Scyld Shefing that opens the poem, and by the knowledge that Sigemund, Beowulf's only peer, dies in his last dragon-fight 'under the grey rock' – a phrase used in setting the scene of Beowulf's last fight. There is a feeling of inevitability as Beowulf goes down before the dragon's third attack. Everything in the poem seems to have foretold this end, and the mythic pattern of the poem requires it. For *Beowulf* is not only a heroic poem and (as I shall argue) an epic, there is also a sense, I suspect, in which it ought to be called a myth. Much of its power, at least, comes from elements which are usually called mythical. Many scholastic angels have feared to tread upon the point of this pin, but I intend to try. It is the monsters that cause the trouble in *Beowulf*, and not only to its hero.

Many of the scholars of the later nineteenth century agreed in recognizing in Beowulf a kind of solar hero and in Grendel a personification of the North Sea or something of the sort.[3]

R. W. Chambers's *Beowulf: An Introduction* gently laid to rest a generation of German mythical interpreters of the poem; the fashion for romantic mythography was passing. Chambers's mentor, W. P. Ker, though likening Beowulf in Denmark to Odysseus in Phaeacia, thought a serious hero should have no truck with monsters, who belong in folk- or fairy-tales. Tolkien persuasively reinstated the monsters at the centre of the poem as incarnations of death and ineradicable evil. Modern literary critics have been shy of the monsters, while generally agreeing with Tolkien. Modern scholars, on the other hand, are steadily Christianizing the interpretation of *Beowulf*; it was recently remarked at a scholarly conference that all were agreed that *Beowulf* was Christian, it was merely a question of whether to put Beowulf in Heaven or in Hell. As a modern reader finishes the poem, this is not (I suspect) the question uppermost in his mind. There is perceptible in much of this 'interpretation' a desire to reduce the poem to a set of *exempla* and moral propositions, or literary sources and rhetorical tropes. The monsters must be explained away as symbols of something else, preferably something rational and definite. Myth-criticism is unfashionable (unlike 'Patristics') because an analogy looks less definite than a literary source.

I am in this introduction concerned with the modern reader's imaginative experience of *Beowulf* as a work of art. This experience is not adequately accounted for by a discussion of literary sources. While the opportunities for fantasy in myth-criticism are obvious, it seems pointless to ignore the evidently superhuman powers attributed to Beowulf: he spends days underwater. The only human enemy he encounters in the poem, Dayraven, he crushes to death with his bare hands; there seems no reason to reject the clue to his bear-like strength offered in the etymology of his name (Bee-Wulf, i.e. Bear). Nor is magic confined to the hero and his monster opponents: the arrival of Scyld, founder of the

Danes, is miraculous, as is his departure. And there are traces in the central story of Beowulf as a wrestling exorcist or as a shaman; even as a mere modern dragon-slayer he kills monsters who live underwater and underground, who can fly in the air and who breathe out fire. He fights at night and in a mythical region of the earth; he receives help from God. The triple pattern of the fights, and their triple internal structure, is also a feature of magic and of folk-poetry. The plot of the Denmark part of the story conforms to the folk-tale known as the Bear's Son tale. To note these 'folk-tale elements', however, is to explain nothing. I believe that Tolkien is right in his view of the poem as a myth and of the monsters as embodying evil. But I think it best to consider the significance of the myth and of the monsters within a larger consideration of *Beowulf* as an epic poem.

An epic, as I see it, should be universal, taking in all of life and representing it in such a way that the general truth of the presentation is universally recognized. Its scope should embrace war and peace, men and gods, life and death in a comprehensive and encyclopædic way. And its presentation should be objective: its scenes, events and characters should form an inter-connected and 'solid' reality, being presented from a consistent and impartial viewpoint.

The note of epic is its objectivity. Northrop Frye argues this strongly:

It is hardly possible to overestimate the importance for Western literature of the *Iliad*'s demonstration that the fall of an enemy, no less than of a friend or leader, is tragic and not comic. With the *Iliad*, once for all, an objective and disinterested element enters into the poet's vision of human life. With this element ... poetry acquires the authority that since the *Iliad* it has never lost, an authority based, like the authority of science, on the vision of nature as an impersonal order.[4]

Aristotle himself seems more specifically interested in the

Introduction

unity than the universality of the *Iliad*. He presents the *Iliad* as having a unity of action, like *Oedipus Rex*, in which everything is subordinated to the central action. But everything that happens in the *Iliad* is not really a consequence of the anger of Achilles, and Aristotle copes with the profusion of episodes by calling the poem *systema polymuthōn*, an organization of many stories.[5] This could also be argued for *Beowulf*. But it seems to me rather that one's consciousness of unity in the *Iliad*, and in epic generally, springs not from a unity of action but a unity of consciousness, an ethos which arises from a primitive intuition of the cosmic solidarity, organic unity and continuity of life. Such a unity of consciousness, found in an oral, public poem, must come from the organic nature of the society that produced it.

Aristotle's emphasis upon the importance of the 'action', the story, of epic, is, however, necessary. The action of an epic, like the action of a myth, should have its own logic and an intrinsic significance. The 'meaning' of the successful return of Odysseus or of Achilles' yielding of the body of Hector to Priam does not need much 'explanation'. It completes a cycle of action of universally obvious significance. The actual progression of the narrative should, in itself, carry the main burden of 'meaning' – as in a religious myth, or in an adventure story. Most rattling good yarns have a skeleton of myth in the cupboard.

If these are the qualities of epic – inclusiveness of scope, objectivity of treatment, unity of ethos and an 'action' of significance – *Beowulf* is not merely a poem about a hero but an epic.

It is inclusive in that it comprehends life and death, peace and war, man and God. The poem begins with the miraculous arrival of the hero Scyld and the founding of the Scylding dynasty and of the Danish people. It ends with the death of the hero Beowulf and the imminent destruction of the Geatish

people. The poem shows the life-cycle of a hero in Beowulf
and of a people in the Danes and the Geats. It shows us
human society at peace in Heorot and at war in Sweden and
elsewhere. Hrothgar's hall, Heorot, is the scene of the sharing
out of food, drink and gold: it is the home of all that is stable
and venerable in human life and society – order, custom,
compliment, ceremony, feasting, poetry, laughter, and the
giving and receiving of treasure and vows. The opening of the
hall is celebrated by the song of a poet who tells of the
Creation:

> There was the music of the harp,
> the clear song of the poet, perfect in his telling
> of the remote first making of man's race.
> He told how, long ago, the Lord formed Earth,
> a plain bright to look on, locked in ocean,
> exulting established the sun and the moon
> as lights to illumine the land-dwellers
> and furnished forth the face of Earth
> with limbs and leaves. Life He then granted
> to each kind of creature that creeps and moves.
>
> (ll. 89–98)

This recital makes it clear that Heorot is a human microcosm
of the divinely created world, the *middanyeard*: 'its radiance,'
we are told, 'lighted the lands of the world.' It is a precinct of
peace, the scene of all the activities which affirm peaceful
values. As for war, apart from full tribal wars (honourable if
regrettable) we have feuds between kindreds and, in the cases
of Unferth, Hrothulf, and Hathkin, within a kindred. Not to
mention the monsters.

As for 'men and gods', *Beowulf* does not keep its cosmos
to the narrowly human level. The 'careless life' of the Danes
within Heorot continues *oth thæt an ongan fyrene fremman,
feond on helle* – 'until One began/To encompass evil, an
enemy from hell'. This evil is given an origin:

> Grendel they called this cruel spirit,
> the fell and fen his fastness was,
> the march his haunt. This unhappy being
> had long lived in the land of monsters
> since the Creator cast them out
> as kindred of Cain. For that killing of Abel
> the everlasting Lord took vengeance.
> There was no joy of that feud: far from mankind
> God drove him out for his deed of shame!
> From Cain came down all kinds misbegotten
> – ogres and elves and evil shades –
> as also the Giants, who joined in long
> wars with God. He gave them their reward.
>
> (ll. 102–14)

Grendel's father is not mentioned; but Hrothgar later warns Beowulf against complacency in prosperity: 'Too close is the slayer/Who shoots the wicked shaft from his bow.' If, as seems likely, this gentleman is the Devil, this is his most open appearance in a poem full of evil and fond of personification. God, however, is present at all crucial points of the action, particularly the monster-fights. Grendel and his mother are descended from the first murderer – the first fratricide, to be precise – and are partly human. The origins and significance of the dragon are more obscure and disputed, as is the question of whether the monsters embody evil, and of what variety. But it is clear that the world of men is set in a cosmic time-scale from the Creation to the destruction of human societies, and in a mythological, metaphysical and perhaps theological scale of beings and of moral values.

Human history also lends scale and scope to *Beowulf*: the rise and fall of both Danish and Geatish races are recorded in some fullness, and we hear the history of the Swedes over three generations, plus some part of that of the Heathobards, Frisians and Franks. This is the historical world of the Baltic and North Seas over the two or three centuries that end the

Age of Migration; and history is supplemented by legend with the figures of Eormenric, Sigemund, the Brisings and Wayland.

The inclusiveness of *Beowulf*'s picture of human life may be impugned on the grounds that it is too aristocratic. The only slave who appears is the thief of the cup from the dragon's hoard. There is some truth but not much force in this objection. The representative method is symbolic not statistical: the whole life of the people and of mankind is involved in the struggle of the hero-king against the dragon. Besides, *Beowulf* is not an irresponsible single-hero romance – it is very much concerned with social ethics.

The second criterion I offered for epic was objectivity. The poem is fair, even sympathetic, to the monsters, but as they are not men their fall cannot be tragic. The opportunity for objectivity of this sort is therefore narrowed. But every single one of the numerous individual human deaths in the poem is given its full weight and significance: the death of Beowulf himself has a full tragic cadence (two dying speeches, two epitaphs, a pyre and a barrow, on the most modest reckoning) but funerals and laments wind in and out of the story. Death, irrespective of nationality, importance or merit, is always accorded due space and honour. Apart from Scyld, Hnæf, Ashhere, Hrethel, the 'last survivor', the hanged man's father, and Beowulf, to name only the most illustrious, the deaths in battle of Geat enemies like Dayraven and Ongentheow are recorded with equally scrupulous fidelity and care. The mad end of Heremod is given dignity; Grendel's victim earns his *wergild*; and the deaths of Sigemund and Hrothgar are eloquent in their omission. Homer and Tolstoy do not outdo *Beowulf* in their respect for the gravity and commonness of dying. Impartial chronicler of these tragedies, the poet nevertheless cannot be said to attain the impersonality of the Homeric voice. Nor can it be said simply, as Aristotle said of Homer, that the poet 'leaves the stage to his personages'.

As well as reporting what he had heard or '*we* have learned', the poet comments frequently; and not all the morals he points are unexceptionable gnomic saws – they are sometimes homiletic, even hortatory. (One or two extreme examples of the latter have been held to be later additions, and although one would wish to keep out the thin end of the wedge of analytic criticism, it is clear why lines such as 183–8 might be felt to violate the unity of tone.) More typical of the poet's exposition is the crucial genealogy provided for Grendel, which has already been cited. When he notes finally that God gave the Giants their reward, there is no mistaking the element of satisfaction in his tone. But this commentary does not vitiate the objectivity of the epic synthesis – on the contrary, it respects it. The human concern is moral, emotional, even anxious; it is certainly very different from the blithe cosmic impartiality of Homer. But the poet's involvement, like Virgil's, does not lead him to disturb the balance of the story: he allows the action to carry the significance of the poem. While remaining outside the poem, he deepens and widens its moral perspective and development, so that it becomes not only *soth* but *sarlic* – like the tale recited by King Hrothgar – not only 'true' but 'grievous'.

Much of the objectivity – the 'truth' – comes from the traditional presentation of life in the heroic world. It is crystallized into generic scenes: voyage, welcome, feast, boast, arming, fight, reward. The exchange of speeches, or of blows, has the traditional and practised feeling of solid simplicity and consistency. The elaborate and time-honoured usages of hospitality by which Beowulf gains Hrothgar's presence and confidence are worth studying from this point of view. There is in fact an element of idealization and standardization. But one is convinced: this is the way things should be conducted in an epic.

Beowulf's arrival and induction is an obvious example of

the self-sustaining order and coherence with which the epic
style invests its imitation of reality. It is easier to pass over the
equally traditional quality of lines like those recording the
death of Grendel's mother:

> She fell to the ground;
> the sword was gory; he was glad at the deed.
>
> (ll. 1568-9)

In which the sword is as much an agent as the man or the
monster. The detachment from the merely human viewpoint,
the standing-back and allowing us to see the incident as a
tableau, marooned in time and space, is surely typical of the
objectivity of epic.

The familiar nuts and bolts of life are presented in stylized,
elevated but simple form. Identities are preserved by rich sets
of names, such as those attached to God, to kings and to
swords. Values are constant: sunlight is good, cold is ominous.
This is not a question of 'imagery' but of reality. The blood
of Grendel's mother

> made the sword dwindle into deadly icicles:
> the war-tool wasted away. It was wonderful indeed
> how it melted away entirely, as the ice does in the spring
> when the Father unfastens the frost's grip,
> unwinds the water's ropes – He who watches over
> the times and the seasons; He is the true God.
>
> (ll. 1606-11)

If names and values are crystallized and standardized in epic
formulae, so are relations: death is represented as sleeping, as
leaving life's feast, as turning away from the courts of men,
as choosing one's bed of slaughter or choosing God's light.
But perhaps the most important stabilizing factor in pre-
serving the epic synthesis is the consistent manner in which
Nature is presented. The stage upon which the human drama
is enacted is large and simple. Men are *hæleth under heofenum*,

'heroes beneath the heavens'; they are *be twæm seonum*, 'between two seas', on *middanyeard*, on 'middle-earth', *swa hit wæter bebugeth*, 'surrounded by water'. We are aware what is above mankind, and what is on either side of it. We are given only the essentials: if Beowulf enters a hall, we know only to whom it belongs, and that his arrival is portentous. His advancing footsteps, slow and heavy, echo through the poem and throughout its universe. The sparks of Beowulf's combat with the dragon 'blaze into the distance'. The watchmen see the boats from afar; Heorot is seen from afar; Beowulf's barrow is seen from afar. Like the 'well-known headlands' of Geatland, the chief realities of the poem heave into view just as and when we expect them to.

This sense of never losing one's bearings is not only spatial but temporal. The coming of day or night or the seasons is never omitted. Likewise we know where every man comes from. Men are *niththa bearn*, 'the children of men'; tribes likewise. A man is identified as someone's son or of someone's kin. For important people or things, complete genealogies or lists of owners are given. Feuds are caused by specific acts. Consequences are no less important than precedences: the nature of the end of every important character is stated or foreshadowed. If races begin, they also end, and the speeches of the 'last survivor' of the race which left the gold of the dragon's hoard and of the messenger who brings the news of Beowulf's death show that peoples, no less than heroes, can be wiped out. Each action in *Beowulf* has a full spatial and temporal dimension, and the cosmic envelope of space and time is always assumed and usually felt to be *there*, immutable. The metaphysical, ethical and moral universe of the poem is also fixed and unalterable in its operations of cause and consequence, origin and end. Evil and good are also strongly, if not always simply, differentiated, as in Wiglaf's speech upbraiding the cowards who did not come to Beowulf's aid.

The operations of nature, time and the cosmos are inescapable, and the consequences of evil human actions scarcely less so. In fact, to speak of nature as an inert stage upon which the human drama is played out is to undervalue nature and over-value human motive in a characteristic modern way. When we are told, at the end of the description of Beowulf's funeral pyre, that 'Heaven swallowed the smoke', whether or not it 'means' that the spirit of Beowulf was accepted by the God of Heaven, Heaven is an agent at least as important as any human actor. The analogy of the drama is misleading. In epic, human and non-human actions are felt to be part of a larger impersonal if organic process, the authority of which is not questioned, but accepted and respected. (Critics of Homer speak of the *aidōs*, or respect, felt for the operations of the process.) Some readers of *Beowulf* may feel that the hand of God (and the finger of the *Beowulf*-poet pointing to the hand of God) is so frequently visible in the world of the poem that it is misleading to regard the cosmic 'process' as truly imper-sonal. 'The lord God then ruled the affairs of men, as He does now,' the poet tells us, and He sees Beowulf right. But there is much reference in the poem to the power of *wyrd* or Fate, sometimes personal, sometimes impersonal. God, for example, does not prevent those who left the gold in the ground from cursing the man who should disturb it. At certain points the poet's bias in favour of some characters (and his horror at Grendel's crimes) is palpable. But the poet, though he doubt-less shapes details of his story and certainly changes its atmos-phere and thematic drift, seems essentially to respect what he has been given by tradition. One of the changes would seem to be an increased sympathy for Grendel: though Beowulf laughs in triumph at Grendel's death (and he is right to do so) it is fated, painful, pitiable and in some way lamentable, despite the assurance that: 'Hell received his heathen soul.' (No tears, however, are shed for Grendel's mother.)

The third criterion, a unity of consciousness, that I suggested for epic, will detain us more briefly. If the reader accepts the second, the consistent objectivity with which the synthesis of the epic world is presented, he is likely to accept the third as a reflection or cause of it. The ethos I find in *Beowulf* is a sense of solidarity with the universe and also of solidarity with the audience. An *aidōs* is felt even towards the inscrutable; as where it is said of the funeral ship that moves out to sea with the body and trappings of Scyld:

> Men under heaven's
> shifting skies, though skilled in counsel,
> cannot say surely who unshipped that cargo.
>
> (ll. 50–52)

Respect of a kind is also felt for Grendel (although Beowulf does not 'count his continued existence/Of the least use to anyone') and for the motives of the slave who stole the dragon's cup, as also for the *casus belli* of the dragon itself. This acceptance of life in all its forms and all its laws must come from the tradition of society. A public poet does not interpret life differently from his audience; and even if the *Beowulf*-poet was a literate Anglian nobleman, a scholar, even a monk, the medium he inherited was traditional, and so was his story. The stability of the system of epic formulae perpetuates the tribal view in the hallowed tribal words. This system is itself an organism. Each verbal formula is the tribe's crystallization of an aspect of experience, and the whole formulaic system might be likened to a polyhedron, a many-faceted lens, through which we see the heroic world – schematically, it may be, but coherently.

But if the epic poet voices the communal view, it is not an undifferentiated or a primitive view. The sensibility through which our *Beowulf* is filtered is not entirely at one with the world it discloses; this is always the case with heroic poetry, which is not composed by heroes. The poet admires, idealizes, identifies with, the epic synthesis and works within its conventions; but he is more reflective, more analytic. The *Beowulf*-poet looks back across the North Sea and knows the world has changed: the Danes, for example, carry out pagan sacrifices.

> Such was their practice,
> a heathen hope
>
> (ll. 178–9)

he notes drily; and explains, with convert indignation and a historian's pride:

> the Maker was unknown to them,
> the Judge of all actions, the Almighty was unheard of,
> they knew not how to praise the Prince of Heaven,
> the Wielder of Glory.
>
> (ll. 180–83)

Unlike his heroes, the poet is a Christian, and the cosmology and aetiology are largely Christianized.[6] A typical Anglo-Saxon moralist, his traditional gnomic gravity and wryness are modified in places by a Christian note of agonized moral and spiritual concern such as we find in the homilies of the time. Where his voice is heard, the poet makes *Beowulf* more of an elegy than a celebration of heroic life, partly because he laments the passing of the heroic virtue of his martial ancestors, partly because he has a horror of war such as might be felt in a settled community in an insecure age. Education has contributed a conscious eloquence and fullness to the epic style which perhaps comes in part from an acquaintance with latin rhetoric. But if the *Beowulf*-poet, in making the *Beowulf*-story into the poem that it is, has deepened it, shaped it and softened it, his consciousness still operates quite naturally in the categories and procedures of the epic tradition. The significance and weight of *Beowulf* lies primarily in the logic of the story and the nature of the style, both traditional, and not in the comments of the poet. Certainly, the moral perspective and an almost Virgilian quality in some of the sentiment cannot be unconnected with Christianity: the audience of the eighth-century *Beowulf* had heard sermons and looked back upon the Age of Migration as their heroic age. To a literate consciousness deepened by Christianity, the heroic world of these heathen ancestors must have seemed doubly admirable and the limitations of heroic life doubly tragic. Unlike some recent commentators who stress the poem's debt to Christianity, I would suggest that what I call the mythic unity of consciousness is supplemented rather than supplanted by the moral and thematic concerns of *Beowulf*'s literary redactor, the *Beowulf*-poet.

A fourth characteristic of epic, I suggested, is that the story should have a kind of self-evident and axiomatic significance. The main story of *Beowulf* is of a hero who braves two life-or-death ordeals against monsters who had killed all previous opponents and dies in a third encounter with a dragon, whom he also succeeds in killing. The three fights are encounters with death in three different shapes (as is the monster-fight in the swimming-match with Breca); they take place in extreme and strange situations where the hero is out of his natural element. This folk-tale may once have been a myth, the three ordeals may have related to rituals in which Beowulf was a shaman passing beyond normal human limits or a culture hero dying to save the dragon's gold representing the grain in the earth – such speculations, if inconclusive, are inevitable. Much of the power of the story comes from this obscure level: but whatever its origins, the main subject of *Beowulf* as it stands is the human challenge to death, and the glorious and tragic potentialities of that challenge. It is quite obvious why we are thrilled by Beowulf's challenge to the dragon:

Passion filled the prince of the Geats:
he allowed a cry to utter from his breast,
roared from his stout heart: as the horn clear in battle
his voice re-echoed through the vault of grey stone.
The hoard-guard recognized a human voice,
and there was no more time for talk of friendship:
hatred stirred. Straightaway
the breath of the dragon billowed from the rock
in a hissing gust; the ground boomed.

(ll. 2550–58)

Much, though by no means all, of the power of *Beowulf* comes from this elemental and basic level, and the mythic quality of such episodes as Scyld's burial, the Grendel-fight, the dive into the mere, and the death and funeral of Beowulf obviously plays a considerable part in the total impression made by the poem.

The 'greatness' of a story, however, does not depend on its theme – man against death – nor on certain big moments: the actual story itself must dramatize the forms of a particular and important human problem. If we analyse the story of *Beowulf* we find that it does not merely consist in the fact that, having defeated two monsters, the hero dies in killing a third.

The epic – as opposed to the merely heroic – potentialities of this story are activated by its relation to the wider theme of human social order. The story of *Beowulf* is not of a hero's fortunes against three monsters but of a hero defending mankind against its enemies. As well as the protagonist and his antagonists there is also a chorus. The story might be represented schematically as on page 32.

If this analysis of the story is right,[7] it would seem to suggest that Beowulf dies not because he is old, still less because he is (as some critics would say) too greedy for gold, but because, now that he is king, no one will fight for him. In all his

Men	Monsters	Hero
A society is founded: Hrothgar in hall		
	Grendel damages hall	
		Beowulf destroys Grendel
Hrothgar in hall		
	Grendel's mother damages hall	
		Beowulf destroys Grendel's mother
Beowulf in hall		
	Dragon destroys hall	
		Beowulf and dragon destroy each other
A society is destroyed		

previous encounters (and this includes the fights with men as well as monster-fights) he is fighting *for* a lord and the lord's people: he volunteers to serve. In his last fight he himself has become lord: he fights for his people, but his people will not fight for him. Had not Wiglaf come to help him he would have died without having killed the dragon. The intervention of Wiglaf produces a resolution: both monster and hero are killed. But humanity, the society of the Geats, now faces complete destruction. The heroic society depends upon the honouring of mutual obligations between lord and thane. As Wiglaf points out to the eleven cowards, the lord distributes mead and arms in peace because he expects the sharers in the feast to share in the fight. If the actual result of the fight is failure, it is at least a glorious and tragic failure. If the heroic code is broken, if the reciprocal obligations are not honoured, then, as Wiglaf puts it to the cowards:

Death is better
for any earl than an existence of disgrace!

It is perhaps not surprising that the values of *Beowulf* should turn out to be those of the classic heroic ethic. But the stress is more upon mutual obligation than on individual glory:

> The bonds of kinship
> nothing may remove for a man who thinks rightly.

The hero was perhaps originally a semi-divine representative of humanity: the Christ of the Anglo-Saxon mystical poem, *The Dream of the Rood*, is a *geong hæleth*, a young hero 'who would set free mankind'.[8] But unless the hero is also a champion, mere heroism is an adolescent ideal – arrogant and irresponsible. The brilliant Achilles is a 'breaker of cities' rather than a 'shepherd of the people'. His glorious life is short, as is that of 'the superb Hygelac', Beowulf's own lord, who falls in a freebooting raid on the Franks. The heroic ideal of unflinching individual courage, of a glorious personal transcendence of human limitations, is always being stalked in *Beowulf* by a complementary ideal of responsibility towards kindred. This second ideal of mutual service between a lord and his people is more honoured in the breach than the observance as the poem wears on.

Thus, Hrothgar the Dane is a patriarchal ruler, an idealized lord like Charlemagne or Arthur, and he and his lady Wealhtheow dispense in Heorot the goods of peace. He is heir to an empire built up by the heroic aggression of the founder, Scyld, whose policy of imperial order and pacification he continues. Like Bede's sparrow passing from darkness to darkness through the lighted hall in the twinkling of an eye, Scyld comes from the sea and returns to the sea. When the stability of the 'careless' life of Heorot is destroyed by the outsider Grendel, Hrothgar is saved by the service of another sea-borne outsider, Beowulf. (Beowulf, like Scyld – and Grendel – is a kind of orphan.) Beowulf purges Heorot of Grendel and his mother; but something is rotten in Denmark still: sitting at Hrothgar's feet is Unferth (or 'Unpeace'), a man who has killed his own kinsmen; Hrothgar's nephew and co-ruler, Hrothulf, brought up like a son, will turn traitor after Hrothgar's death and kill his sons and heirs; and Hrothgar is to marry his daughter, Freawaru, to Ingeld the Heathobard in what Beowulf grimly foresees will be a vain effort to heal the tribal feud, which in its last outbreak will lead both to the burning-down of Heorot and the end of the Heathobards.

At home in Geatland – to pursue this 'social' theme – Beowulf gives all his prizes to his lord Hygelac, with the thane-like words:

> I rejoice to present them. Joy, for me, always
> lies in your gift. Little family
> do I have in the world, Hygelac, besides yourself.
>
> (ll. 2149–51)

After Hygelac's calamitous death, his nephew Beowulf serves his son Heardred, and assumes the kingdom only when there is no one else to do so (the contrast with Hrothulf is marked). He protects his people fifty years, and gives Wiglaf his dying voice. But Beowulf, son of an exiled murderer, is pointedly not given a son: he is unique. The gold he won for his people – the embodied glory of a whole race of men – is returned to the ground 'as useless to men as it was before'. No one shall inherit: the gold and the glory are buried with him.

The cycle of the heroic life would then seem, in a paradigm, to run as follows: young founders, builders and defenders (Scyld, Hrothgar, Beowulf) enjoy a brief prosperity, but in old age the 'troops of friends' are not enough, or cannot be relied on. The warlike get killed (Hygelac, Ongentheow), the peaceable eventually fall through accident, treachery or frailty (Hrethel, Hrothgar, Beowulf). The end of the heroic age is shown through the plot (finally, the failure of the young companions) and through the modification of the ideal hero from the adventurer Sigemund to the relatively *pius* Beowulf.

The epitaph remembers him as gentle, gracious and kind – *monna mildust*, 'the mildest of men', as well as being *lofgeornost*. For a northern hero, Beowulf is ceremonious, eloquent, courteous, modest, almost urbane. It is only when taunted by the egregious Unferth that he boasts of his swimming-match with Breca. And he returns the sword that Unferth had lent him for the fight against Grendel's mother with gracious thanks, making no mention of the fact that in the fight it had failed him completely. (Wiglaf, likewise, when reporting the dragon-fight conceals the decisiveness of his own intervention.) Beowulf, in fact, is a very gentle bear – an ideal hero, but also an ideal thane and lord. His death, though tragic, is glorious, like that of Bryhtnoth at Maldon. When he was young his companions had stood by him – unnecessarily – but at home, in old age, he is deserted by them. He had wasted his armour on them, says Wiglaf. The days of heroism are over.

I have tried to show that if the characteristics of epic are inclusiveness of range, objectivity of treatment, unity of ethos and a significant action, then *Beowulf* may fairly be called an epic. If the reader is not much impressed by this honourable title of Epic, I hope at least that he may find in *Beowulf* a breadth and depth, a resonance and dignity that he might not expect to find in a glorified folk-tale full of interesting historical material, which is how the poem is often presented. One could express the poem's apprehension of a deeper reality by saying that the life and death of the hero recapitulates the life-cycle of the race: the heroic generation is born, flourishes and dies. Onto the elemental power of the original tale (or myth) the teller has grafted a set of human and social themes, so that the single-handed 'adventure' comes to express the struggle of the forces of life and death in human society and human nature, and the monsters become malign embodiments of extrapolated human evil.

The struggle of the *aglæcas* ('terrible ones' – a name given to Beowulf as well as to the monsters) is paralleled throughout by the struggle of the forces of harmony and the forces of destruction. This conflict first manifests itself powerfully with the coming of Grendel, but there are auguries of his coming in the apparently laudatory recital of the founding of the Scylding dynasty; we learn that Scyld took away the mead-benches of terrified local tribes; that the 'lordless' Danes themselves had been quite unprotected before his coming; and immediately after the first feast in Heorot we have a veiled allusion to the burning-down of 'the world's palace' in the last outbreak of the Heathobard feud. The serene hymn of the Caedmon-like poet to the creative achievement of Heorot, an indoor Eden, a *yeard* within the *middanyeard*, seems almost to provoke the irruption of Grendel into the poem.

> So the company of men led a careless life,
> all was well with them: until One began
> to encompass evil, an enemy from hell . . .
>
> (ll. 99–101)

All the warmth and light which has gone into the description of Heorot immediately reappears with horrific intensity in the description of Grendel. This reversal and this dualism is most marked in the structure and the dynamics of the poem, as we shall see. But even before Grendel appears we have become acquainted with evil and pain in Scyld's ripped-out mead-benches, the desolation of the lordless Danes, Scyld's death and the treacherous burning-down of Heorot; good and evil are intertwined from the beginning of the poem, and Grendel appears as the emanation of all those envious forces within and without humanity which are driven to destroy the unendurable music and laughter of Heorot.

Opposition and dualism work throughout the poem: the attraction and repulsion between the positive and negative poles can be felt in its every part – not only between God and the demons, the hero and the monsters, the true and the false thane, but in all its values, movement and imagery. The values of the poem are similar to those of *Macbeth*: light, feasting, order and ceremony on the one hand, darkness, murder, disorder and savagery on the other – 'You have displaced the mirth, broke the good meeting/With most admired disorder.' The public celebration of social unity is the sharing out at the feast of food, drink, gold and, above all, of words: its anti-thesis is Grendel's grinding-up of his enemies, uncooked, in silent, solitary, nocturnal, cannibalistic joy. The after-dinner conversation of the birds and beasts of carrion on the battle-field is another repulsive anti-type of the feast of life. Such violent oppositions, contrasts and comparisons can be found at every stage of the poem. The first of them, the *wrestling* of Beowulf and Grendel, powerfully suggests things beyond itself:

> Fear entered into
> the listening North Danes, as that noise rose up again
> strange and strident. It shrilled terror
> to the ears that heard it through the hall's side-wall,
> the grisly plaint of God's enemy,
> his song of ill-success, the sobs of the damned one
> bewailing his pain.
>
> (ll. 782–8)

Previously, we have felt Grendel's hatred and rage at hearing the song of Creation through the same walls. In places the paralleling and pairing can seem a little schematic, as in the elaborate exclamations over the double death of hero and dragon. But this elaboration and orchestration of the primitive conflict of Beowulf and Grendel into an epic conflict between life and death, harmony and chaos, good and evil, is the poet's chief work. This thematic development is evidently conscious: the tracing of Grendel's envy and hatred back to Cain's fratricide and the Giants' rebellion involves a theory of evil. The *morthor-hete*, the murderous hatred of individuals and of tribes, takes on the pattern of an apparently inextinguishable and tragic blood-feud within the family of the children of men. The duty to avenge a slain kinsman is absolute; even Grendel's mother seems to receive some sympathy for her vengeance-raid. Property and territorial rights are almost as sacred: great stress is laid on the ownership of land, halls, cups and armour. The stolen drinking-cup belongs to the last survivor of the race who buried it, and to the dragon, its appointed guardian. Even Grendel may receive pity as a disinherited exile, an outcast from life's feast only by inheritance of blood. These iron laws of motive and necessary effect bind the action of *Beowulf*. Beowulf himself swears no unrightful oaths; but he feels obliged to help the exiled Eadgils to his vengeance. There's no doubt the poem is, in one sense, 'about' treacherous fratricide versus firm friendship; in this focus on the tragic consequences of the unappeasable feud *Beowulf* is traditionally Germanic. But the question 'Am I my brother's keeper?' is becoming more insistent.

Another focus of the poem, upon the destruction of whole societies, symbolized by the empty and silent hall, is traditional in Old English poetry. Elegies such as *The Ruin* and *The Wanderer* are affected by Christian ideas of the transitoriness of this world and its imminent end; but the scholars who collect examples of 'the *ubi sunt* formula' do not seem to notice that here the tone is more one of sorrowful lament that these heroic glories are now past, than of confidence in the heavenly remedy. (The same grief is felt in the Welsh

Gododdin and in the lament for Cynddylan's hall; and one does not have to be a Christian to feel that life is short and that the world may come to an end.[9])

The *Beowulf*-poet constantly connects the nightmare of the empty hall with the destructiveness of the blood-feud, and in his critique of heroic society there is a Christian element, shown in the ideal of a more god-fearing, responsible and civilized hero. There is also some Christian influence in the poet's rather confusing comments on the dragon's gold, but Beowulf's desire to fight the dragon alone, however tragic in its consequences, is necessary and admirable in a hero. Grief and admiration are mixed equally as they are in the case of Bryhtnoth in *The Battle of Maldon*. The emphasis is not upon individual morality but upon *wyrd*, the inevitable pattern of things.

This introduction does not claim to offer an 'interpretation' of *Beowulf*, and I would not care to go further in this direction, except to say that those who see it as a consistently Christian poem, unless they take up the crystal ball of allegory, must find their case seriously hindered by the lack of Christian reference after Beowulf's return to Geatland. The poet has made overtly missionary comments on Danish idol-worship and on God's mastery of human affairs, and he has inspired Hrothgar to deliver a homily to Beowulf about pride; why then does he fail to point the morals of events in Geatland?

This last point brings into consideration the difference in character between the Danish and Geatish halves of the poem, and the thorny question of the genesis, composition and transmission of *Beowulf*. Nothing but convenience recommends the uncritical assumption of many critics that the eighth-century 'original' (itself two centuries and an unknown number of stages behind our manuscript) was the 'original' work of a single literary author. The poem falls into two halves, the second much different in structure and content.

It seems thinner: it contains, for example, next to no picture of life at court, a confusing number of new motifs, and much more prophecy and reminiscence than narrative. The work retains, as a whole, a decided thematic unity, but there is some reason to suppose that the two halves were originally separate tales, and that Beowulf's repetitions to Hrothgar and to Hygelac of the fight at the Mere and of the whole Danish adventure respectively are 'oral' repeats. Like Odysseus' accounts of his adventures, they vary interestingly from the poet's first account – and this inconsistency, too, is a regular feature of orally composed works.

Many critics with textual and editorial training (or, alternatively, the assumptions of modern literary criticism) ignore suggestions that the poem is anything other than a fixed and unique literary document, the product of painstaking revision and conflation, from a pen wielded by someone perhaps not unlike themselves; smelling respectably of the lamp. To all the evidence of Parry and his followers they reply with aplomb that someone must have written the poem down, and proceed to treat it like any other piece of dead literature. Evidence of any stylistic or thematic parallels between *Beowulf* and other literary texts of the period suggests to these diffusionists the kind of 'literary influence' familiar in later periods of literature. Since the majority of works surviving from the eighth century and before are naturally the works of Latin Christianity, *Beowulf* is assimilated to that model. And since most of the authors, especially of sermons, use a rhetorical style, *Beowulf* is seen as a work in the same style. Literary rhetoric and oral composition, of course, have in common many techniques designed to aid extempore improvisation and declamation – they both use procedures of amplification and variation upon a typical theme. If 'the *Beowulf*-poet' is anything like what he is commonly conceived to be, he had heard and even read sermons and saints' lives, and had learned

from their techniques – as did the illiterate neatherd, Caed-
mon, whom Bede presents as our first Christian poet.[10] But,
like the illiterate Caedmon, 'the *Beowulf*-poet' could never
have begun to compose unless he had had an oral vernacular
poetic tradition of totally different origin from rhymed Latin
hymns or Silver Latin elegiacs. It was this Germanic tradition
of oral heroic verse composition that supplied him with his
repertoire of themes and narrative devices and verbal for-
mulae – essentially, I would suggest, it supplied him, not just
with a *Beowulf*-kit, but with the *Beowulf*-poem in oral form. It
is now a written poem, not an oral one. But a written oral
poem, like a film of a play, only makes sense when the con-
ventions of the original are understood.

This is not the place to try to sum up Parry's celebrated
thesis about oral poetry. It is based upon a rigorous analysis of
Homer's style and a comparison with the techniques of mod-
ern Yugoslav oral epic improvisation. He demonstrates that
the Homeric poems are entirely composed of formulaic
phrases and shows that the illiterate Yugoslav poets have a
repertoire of verbal formulae, narrative schemas and type-
scenes which enables them to improvise freely and create
monumentally large stories in verse. The stories, entirely
traditional in matter and manner, are nevertheless improvised
and not memorized. Parry's thesis, which has never seriously
been challenged though it was ignored in some quarters,
destroys the supposition that non-literates could not possibly
have created the Homeric epics. The full implications for the
criticism of Homer are still being developed.[11]

Parry's approach has been applied by other Harvard
scholars to other early literatures, including Old English. The
percentage of Homeric lines which is composed of formulae
is almost one hundred; it is much smaller for Old English
poems, but still considerable. *Beowulf* also shows many signs
of oral narrative composition: it has type-scenes which are

themselves narrative formulae – the banquet, the battle, the boast, the voyage, the funeral – and its whole structure conforms to the typologies of folk-lore. An introduction to a translation is not the place, as I say, to embark upon a proper statement of the 'oral' approach, with its formidable problems and complexities; but I shall partly draw upon this approach in the brief concluding description of the structure and style of *Beowulf*.

My presentation of *Beowulf* as three monster-fights supported by a set of stories about feuds may seem misleadingly simple and diagrammatic to someone reading the poem for the first time. Even if one is prepared to trust that the poem will gradually reveal its thematic coherence, the bearing of many of the 'digressions' may not be at all obvious when one is reading it through. But these digressions are really expanded allusions, and in any decent allusion there is a certain riddling delight in making the point at issue not too obvious. A more crucial matter is the whole narrative method of *Beowulf*. To those who are accustomed to action in their epics, *Beowulf* may seem something of an oratorio. Even the Grendel-fight cannot compare with the corresponding Glam-fight in *Grettissaga*; the only passage of conventionally exciting action is the Hygelac-Ongentheow episode. Compared with a modern thriller, *Beowulf* is slow, lacking in suspense, full of speeches and of asides from the author. It is aural rather than visual. It is as much a meditation upon an action as an action. And, even more than most works, it only makes full sense if one considers it synchronically as well as diachronically – that is, if one follows it not only as a single series of events in time but also thinks of it as a pattern of events occurring simultaneously and forming a larger pattern. *Beowulf*, in fact, is full of anticipations, comparisons and flashbacks, which lend its events not just a profile but a fullness and roundness, because they are in a sense complete before they begin. The life of

Heorot is an example we have looked at: it is burned down almost before it is built. And it might be said of Scyld, as of the Thane of Cawdor, that nothing in his life became him like the leaving of it.

This habit of regarding everything in the narrative as if it had already happened and the results were only too well-known is typical of traditional poetry: we are told the results of all three monster-fights not only in advance but several times afterwards as well. Time is irrelevant: Beowulf ages fifty years in one line, and when we are told of the by-passed events of Geatish history it is in an order more thematic than chronological. Again, immediately *Beowulf*'s fifty-year reign has flashed by, we are told how the dragon's hoard is robbed before we know how either gold or dragon got there. The important thing is to exhibit the combatants to the audience at the opening of the proceedings.

The tales being largely familiar, the interest of the audience is obviously all in the telling and in the parallels. They seem to have liked artful elaboration and fullness in banquets and speeches and armour; but action is presented less by visual particulars than by means of its material effects – often sound effects. There is a consistent metonymy: we hear the footsteps of Beowulf, the scream of Grendel, the horn of Hygelac, the jingle of a mail-shirt. It would be easier to imagine *Beowulf* as an oratorio than as a Kurosawa film.

Indirectness and metaphor are endemic in the poetic style. The sun is 'the sky's candle' or 'heaven's jewel'; Beowulf is 'Hygelac's thane' or 'Hrothgar's monster-warden'; the dragon is 'the barrow's guardian' or 'night's alone-flier'; God is 'glory's wielder' or 'victory's bestower'. This habit of providing alternative names in the form of a genitive relation between two other nouns, often images, is conventionally praised for its vividness ('swan's riding' or 'whale's acre' as kennings for the sea), but the vividness is generally intellectual rather than visual or imagistic or 'concrete'. To refer to battle as 'the sword-play' is characteristically Anglo-Saxon: it abstracts and schematizes, it disguises and elevates. The painful confusion of battle is, by an ironic euphemism, transformed into a game of objects, beautiful and bloodless. Paradoxically, this devious and euphemistic stress on effects can, by leaving so much to the imagination, intensify the reality of what is being described – or half-described.

Wiglaf's speech over Beowulf's body exemplifies all these characteristics:

> 'Now the flames shall grow dark
> and the fire destroy the sustainer of the warriors
> who often endured the iron shower
> when, string-driven, the storm of arrows
> sang over shield-wall, and the shaft did its work
> urged on by feathers, furthered the arrow-head.'
>
> (ll. 3114–19)

The audience evidently took pleasure in the elaboration, even the perversity, of these attempts to avoid the obvious. Laconic understatement and the use of the negative accomplish the same purpose. Wiglaf says

> 'little courtesy was shown in allowing me to pass
> beneath the earth-wall'   (ll. 3089–90)

whereas in fact, as we know, he had to kill the dragon to get inside. This grim kind of humour, still to be found in Yorkshire, is observable in a more weighty and elaborate form in this comment on the dragon's first blitz upon the Geats:

> That was a fearful beginning
> for the people of that country; uncomfortable and swift
> was the end to be likewise for their lord and treasure-giver!
>
> (ll. 2309–11)

'As the beginning was to the people so the end would be to their lord' – this feeling for parallelism and antithesis is also very typical of *Beowulf.*

Parallelism, antithesis and variation are the characteristics of the verbal style of *Beowulf,* which is considerably more embellished and involved than that of other Old English poetry. The syntax is correspondingly more sustained; but the 'lack of steady advance' Klaeber noted in the narrative is even more marked in the sentence. Traditional near-synonyms are juggled in dense apposition, so that the 'advance', always slow, is almost suspended. Thus:

> Then Beowulf spoke; bent by smith's skill
> the meshed rings of his mailshirt glittered.

(ll. 405–6)

or

> 'To you I will now
> put one request, Royal Scylding,
> Shield of the South Danes, one sole favour
> that you'll not deny me, dear lord of your people,
> now that I have come this far, Fastness of Warriors;
> that I alone may be allowed with my loyal and determined
> crew of companions, to cleanse your hall Heorot.'

(ll. 426–32)

The variation and parallelism of the poetic style distinguish it from that of Homer. One of Parry's criteria for the 'orality' of a style was that there should be no duplication of formulae; that for any given essential idea, in any given metrical position and grammatical form, there should be one formula and one only. Though a great number of formulae are recurrent (such as 'Beowulf spoke', 'protector of the people', 'heroes under heaven', 'grim and greedy', 'giver of rings' and 'hard under helmet') more of them are not: profusion rather than economy is the rule for synonyms and epithets. This is perhaps because it is easier to compose in Old English metre than in Greek

dactylic hexameters, possibly because of the influence of
literary rhetoric, and certainly because of something in the
Anglo-Saxon temperament. The effect is much less simple,
rapid and direct than Homer. There are simple half-lines: 'He
was a good king'; 'he chose his deathbed'; 'the journey was
over' – but they seem to be used for contrast with the ante-
cedent amplitude. Thus, of the dragon:

He had poured out fire and flame on the people,
he had put them to the torch; he trusted now to the barrow's walls
and to his fighting strength; his faith misled him.

(ll. 2321–3)

Many an eloquent verse-paragraph concludes with a pithy,
often ironic, comment of this sort, and the contrast of elabora-
tion and plainness, of raising up and knocking down, is
marked. The way the sentences writhe, twist and twine back
on themselves is reminiscent of the wrestling beasts so com-
mon in Anglo-Saxon art: the eye is teased and bewildered by
the fantastic convolutions of these abstract ribbon-like crea-
tures that suddenly end in a mean, jewelled head and reveal
themselves, not as a maze or a Celtic version of a Greek key,
but as serpents.

The denseness and allusiveness of *Beowulf*'s style are chiefly
created by diction. The nouns and adjectives which make up
most of the epic formulae are highly poetical – not only
imaginative and beautiful but far-fetched and peculiar to
poetry; they often contain a fossilized animistic metaphor.
The vocabulary (and word-order) of Old English prose is
simpler and more analytic. The traditional and stylized quality
of the poetic diction is difficult to convey in translation with-
out recourse to archaism. The Old English diction is special
and archaic but not archaizing and the effect is of a strenuous
and untiring eloquence rather than of a mellifluous rhetoric:
Milton rather than Spenser. The expression 'poetic diction'

may still suggest something attenuated and tame, but in his odes Wordsworth used a style different from that of his lyrical ballads. Staleness or sameness are absent from *Beowulf*, whose variety continually exercises the mind.

The verbal vigour of the epic cannot be separated from the movement of the verses. The key to Old English metre is the caesura in the middle of the line: the two halves of the line on either side of the break are felt to be equal in weight. Each half-line normally consists of a phrase containing two stressed and two or more unstressed syllables. (The basis of the metre is stress or accent, not the quantity nor the number of the syllables.) Each half-line, consisting normally of two stressed and two unstressed syllables, has an internal balance; and itself is balanced against the other half-line. A typical line might be:

the fell and fen his fastness was. (l. 104)

A line therefore consists of two units which are ultimately identical in their general metrical form:

$$\times \, / \mid \times \, / \parallel \times \, / \mid \times \, /$$

although, ignoring stress, the most common distribution of syllables into phrases actually occurring in *Beowulf* is:

$$\times \mid \times\times\times \parallel \times\times\times \mid \times \ [12]$$

The Old English metre is often called 'the alliterative measure', especially when it re-emerges in the thirteenth century, by which time it has lost its true character. The alliteration, though a compulsory and distinctive feature, is less fundamental than the stress pattern which it serves to reinforce. The rule is that the first letter of the first stressed syllable in the second half-line must also begin one of the two stressed syllables in the first half-line. The other stressed syllable in the first half-line may alliterate; the last stressed syllable in the line must not. Thus, of the four stresses in the line, the first and/or the second must alliterate with the third, and the fourth must be different. Only the four fully-stressed syllables of the line enter into this calculation, and it is necessary to distinguish a fully-stressed from a half-stressed syllable. All vowels alliterate. This account ignores the refinements of the system which deal with extra syllables and stresses and missing syllables and stresses. The essence of the metre is the theoretical norm: 'two is to two as two is to two', where the 'twos' represent two syllables, one stressed, the other not. All the actual lines that occur are variations on this very symmetrical norm. The alliteration binds the half-lines together over the break and emphasizes this symmetry. The stressed syllables are also, needless to say, the most important syllables from the point of view of the sense.

The sentences are built up of formulaic phrases, each half a line long, and the sense, as Milton prescribed for 'true musical delight', is 'variously drawn out from one verse into another'. Traditional oral composition by phrase accounts for an exclamatory lack of syntactic subordination and for the tacking, eddying, resumptive movement of the sense.

The pleasure of Anglo-Saxon verse, as with most verse, is of variety in unity, freedom within form: it arises from the play between the demands of the sense and the demands of the metre. The symmetry of the halves of the line produces balance, antithesis and chiasmos much more commonly than in unrhymed iambic pentameter, and the forward movement is much more impeded than in later English blank verse. The halves of the line are, as often as not, out of the natural sequence of prose or spoken syntax, and, as the mind re-shuffles the parts of the sentence, the tendency of the half-lines is to move apart; but the alliteration and the stress pattern bind them together. The final impression of the verse in *Beowulf*, then, is of contrasting energies being held in a rhythmic balance – and this is also the impression given by the poem as a whole.

A word on verse translation. Just as some modern readers may find this version too slavish, there will be others more learned than myself who may find it too free. I would ask them, as scholars, to consider whether a literal prose version of a verse epic is, properly, a translation.

Old English *scopas*, or poets, are represented as composing to the harp, and the poetry was therefore chanted or sung. While I cannot expect readers to sing, I hope they will read the verse aloud. *Beowulf* was not written to be readable but to be listened to.

BEOWULF

Attend!
We have heard of the thriving of the throne of Denmark,
how the folk-kings flourished in former days,
how those royal athelings earned that glory.

Was it not *Scyld Shefing* that shook the halls,
took mead-benches, taught encroaching
foes to fear him – who, found in childhood,
lacked clothing? Yet he lived and prospered,
grew in strength and stature under the heavens
until the clans settled in the sea-coasts neighbouring
over the whale-road all must obey him
and give tribute. He was a good king!

A boy child was afterwards born to Scyld,
a young child in hall-yard, a hope for the people,
sent them by God; the griefs long endured
were not unknown to Him, the harshness of years
without a lord. Therefore the Life-bestowing
Wielder of Glory granted them this blessing.
Through the northern lands the name of Beow,
the son of Scyld, sprang widely.
For in youth an atheling should so use his virtue,
give with a free hand while in his father's house,
that in old age, when enemies gather,
established friends shall stand by him
and serve him gladly. It is by glorious action
that a man comes by honour in any people.

At the hour shaped for him Scyld departed,
the hero crossed into the keeping of his Lord.

They carried him out to the edge of the sea,
his sworn arms-fellows, as he had himself desired them
while he wielded his words, Warden of the Scyldings,
beloved folk-founder; long had he ruled.

A boat with a ringed neck rode in the haven,
icy, out-eager, the atheling's vessel,
and there they laid out their lord and master,
dealer of wound gold, in the waist of the ship,
in majesty by the mast. A mound of treasures
from far countries was fetched aboard her,
and it is said that no boat was ever more bravely fitted out
with the weapons of a warrior, war accoutrement,
swords and body-armour; on his breast were set
treasures and trappings to travel with him
on his far faring into the flood's sway.

This hoard was not less great than the gifts he had had
from those who at the outset had adventured him
over seas, alone, a small child.

High over head they hoisted and fixed
a gold *signum*; gave him to the flood,
let the seas take him, with sour hearts
and mourning mood. Men under heaven's
shifting skies, though skilled in counsel,
cannot say surely who unshipped that cargo.

Then for a long space there lodged in the stronghold
Beowulf the Dane, dear king of his people,
famed among nations – his father had taken
leave of the land – when late was born to him
the lord Healfdene, lifelong the ruler
and war-feared patriarch of the proud Scyldings.
He next fathered four children

that leaped into the world, this leader of armies,
Heorogar and *Hrothgar* and Halga the Good;
and Ursula, I have heard, who was Onela's queen,
knew the bed's embrace of the Battle-Scylfing.

Then to Hrothgar was granted glory in battle,
mastery of the field; so friends and kinsmen
gladly obeyed him, and his band increased
to a great company. It came into his mind
that he would command the construction
of a huge mead-hall, a house greater
than men on earth ever had heard of,
and share the gifts God had bestowed on him
upon its floor with folk young and old –
apart from public land and the persons of slaves.
Far and wide (as I heard) the work was given out
in many a tribe over middle earth,
the making of the mead-hall. And, as men reckon,
the day of readiness dawned very soon
for this greatest of houses. *Heorot* he named it
whose word ruled a wide empire.
He made good his boast, gave out rings,
arm-bands at the banquet. Boldly the hall reared
its arched gables; unkindled the torch-flame
that turned it to ashes. The time was not yet
when the blood-feud should bring out again
sword-hatred in sworn kindred.

It was with pain that the powerful spirit
dwelling in darkness endured that time,
hearing daily the hall filled
with loud amusement; there was the music of the harp,
the clear song of the poet, perfect in his telling
of the remote first making of man's race.
He told how, long ago, the Lord formed Earth,

a plain bright to look on, locked in ocean,
exulting established the sun and the moon
as lights to illumine the land-dwellers
and furnished forth the face of Earth
with limbs and leaves. Life He then granted
to each kind of creature that creeps and moves.

So the company of men led a careless life,
all was well with them: until One began
to encompass evil, an enemy from hell.
Grendel they called this cruel spirit,
the fell and fen his fastness was,
the march his haunt. This unhappy being
had long lived in the land of monsters
since the Creator cast them out
as kindred of *Cain*. For that killing of Abel
the eternal Lord took vengeance.
There was no joy of that feud: far from mankind
God drove him out for his deed of shame!
From Cain came down all kinds misbegotten
– ogres and elves and evil shades –
as also the Giants, who joined in long
wars with God. He gave them their reward.

With the coming of night came Grendel also,
sought the great house and how the Ring-Danes
held their hall when the horn had gone round.
He found in Heorot the force of nobles
slept after supper, sorrow forgotten,
the condition of men. Maddening with rage,
he struck quickly, creature of evil:
grim and greedy, he grasped on their pallets
thirty warriors, and away he was out of there,
thrilled with his catch: he carried off homeward
his glut of slaughter, sought his own halls.

As the day broke, with the dawn's light
Grendel's outrage was openly to be seen:
night's table-laughter turned to morning's
lamentation. Lord Hrothgar
sat silent then, the strong man mourned,
glorious king, he grieved for his thanes
as they read the traces of a terrible foe,
a cursed fiend. That was too cruel a feud,
too long, too hard!
                 Nor did he let them rest
but the next night brought new horrors,
did more murder, manslaughter and outrage
and shrank not from it: he was too set on these things.

It was not remarked then if a man looked
for sleeping-quarters quieter, less central,
among the outer buildings; now openly shown,
the new hall-thane's hatred was manifest
and unmistakable. Each survivor
then kept himself at safer distance.

So Grendel became ruler; against right he fought,
one against all. Empty then stood
the best of houses, and for no brief space;
for twelve long winters torment sat
on the Friend of the Scyldings, fierce sorrows
and woes of every kind; which was not hidden
from the sons of men, but was made known
in grieving songs, how Grendel warred
long on Hrothgar, the harms he did him
through wretched years of wrong, outrage
and persecution. Peace was not in his mind
towards any companion of the court of Hrothgar,
the feud was not abated, the blood-price was unpaid.
Nor did any counsellor have cause to look for

a bright man-price at the murderer's hand:
the dark death-shadow drove always against them,
old and young; abominable
he watched and waited for them, walked nightlong
the misty moorland. Men know not
where hell's familiars fleet on their errands!

Again and again the enemy of man
stalking unseen, struck terrible
and bitter blows. In the black nights
he camped in the hall, under Heorot's gold roof;
yet he could not touch the treasure-throne
against the Lord's will, whose love was unknown to him.
A great grief was it for the Guardian of the Scyldings,
crushing to his spirit. The council lords
sat there daily to devise some plan,
what might be best for brave-hearted
Danes to contrive against these terror-raids.
They prayed aloud, promising sometimes
on the altars of their idols unholy sacrifices
if the Slayer of souls would send relief
to the suffering people.

        Such was their practice,
a heathen hope; Hell possessed
their hearts and minds: the Maker was unknown to them,
the Judge of all actions, the Almighty was unheard of,
they knew not how to praise the Prince of Heaven,
the Wielder of Glory.

        Woe to him who must
in terrible trial entrust his soul
to the embrace of the burning, banished from thought
of change or comfort! Cheerful the man
able to look to the Lord at his death-day,
to find peace in the Father's embrace!

This season rocked the son of Healfdene
with swingeing sorrows; nor could the splendid man
put his cares from him. Too cruel the feud,
too strong and long-lasting, that struck that people,
a wicked affliction, the worst of nightmares!

This was heard of at his home by one of *Hygelac*'s followers,
a good man among the Geats, Grendel's raidings;
he was for main strength of all men foremost
that trod the earth at that time of day;
build and blood matched.

                 He bade a seaworthy
wave-cutter be fitted out for him; the warrior king
he would seek, he said, over swan's riding,
that lord of great name, needing men.
The wiser sought to dissuade him from voyaging
hardly or not at all, though they held him dear;
they whetted his quest-thirst, watched omens.
The prince had already picked his men
from the folk's flower, the fiercest among them
that might be found. With fourteen men
he sought sound-wood; sea-wise *Beowulf*
led them right down to the land's edge.

Time running on, she rode the waves now,
hard in by headland. Harnessed warriors
stepped on her stem; setting tide churned
sea with sand, soldiers carried
bright mail-coats to the mast's foot,
war-gear well-wrought; willingly they shoved her out,
thorough-braced craft, on the craved voyage.

Away she went over a wavy ocean,
boat like a bird, breaking seas,
wind-whetted, white-throated,

till the curved prow had ploughed so far
– the sun standing right on the second day –
that they might see land loom on the skyline,
then the shimmer of cliffs, sheer fells behind,
reaching capes.

        The crossing was at an end;
closed the wake. Weather-Geats
stood on strand, stepped briskly up;
a rope going ashore, ring-mail clashed,
battle-girdings. God they thanked
for the smooth going over the salt-trails.

The watchman saw them. From the wall where he stood,
posted by the Scyldings to patrol the cliffs,
he saw the polished lindens pass along the gangway
and the clean equipment. Curiosity
moved him to know who these men might be.

Hrothgar's thane, when his horse had picked
its way down to the shore, shook his spear
fiercely at arm's length, framed the challenge:
'Strangers, you have steered this steep craft
through the sea-ways, sought our coast.
I see you are warriors; you wear that dress now.
I must ask who you are.

        In all the years
I have lived as look-out at land's end here
– so that no foreigners with a fleet-army
might land in Denmark and do us harm –
shield-carriers have never come ashore
more openly. You had no assurance
of welcome here, word of leave
from Hrothgar and *Hrothulf*!

                              I have not in my life
set eyes on a man with more might in his frame
than this helmed lord. He's no hall-fellow
dressed in fine armour, or his face belies him;
he has the head of a hero.

                              I'll have your names now
and the names of your fathers; or further you shall not go
as undeclared spies in the Danish land.
Stay where you are, strangers, hear
what I have to say! Seas crossed,
it is best and simplest straightaway to acknowledge
where you are from, why you have come.'

The captain gave him a clear answer,
leader of the troop, unlocked his word-hoard:
'We here are come from the country of the Geats
and are King Hygelac's hearth-companions.
My noble father was known as Edgetheow,
a front-fighter famous among nations,
who had seen many seasons when he set out at last
an old man from the halls; all the wiser men
in the world readily remember him.

    It is with loyal and true intention that we come
to seek your lord the son of Healfdene,
guardian of the people: guide us well therefore!
We have a great errand to the glorious hero,
the Shepherd of the Danes; the drift of it
shall not be kept from you. You must know if indeed
there is truth in what is told in Geatland,
that among the Scyldings some enemy,
an obscure assailant in the opaque night-times,
makes spectacles of spoil and slaughter
in hideous feud. To Hrothgar I would
openheartedly unfold a plan

how the old commander may overcome his foe;
if indeed an easing is ever to slacken
these besetting sorrows, a settlement
when chafing cares shall cool at last.
Otherwise he must miserably live out
this lamentable time, for as long as Heorot,
best of houses, bulks to the sky.'

The mounted coastguard made reply,
unshrinking officer: 'A sharp-witted man,
clear in his mind, must be skilled
to discriminate deeds and words.
I accept what I am told, that this troop is loyal
to the Scyldings' Protector. Pass forward with your
weapons and war-dress! I am willing to guide you,
commanding meanwhile the men under me
to guard with care this craft of yours,
this new-tarred boat at its berth by our strand
against every enemy until again it bear
its beloved captain over the current sea,
curve-necked keel, to the coasts of the Geat;
such a warrior shall be accorded
unscathed passage through the shocks of battle.'

The vessel was still as they set forward,
the deep-chested ship, stayed at its mooring,
fast at its anchor. Over the cheek-pieces
boar-shapes shone out, bristling with gold,
blazing and fire-hard, fierce guards
of their bearers' lives. Briskly the men went
marching together, making out at last
the ample eaves adorned with gold:
to earth's men the most glorious
of houses under heaven, the home of the king;
its radiance lighted the lands of the world.

The coastguard showed them the shining palace,
the resort of heroes, and how they might
rightly come to it; this captain in the wars
then brought his horse about, and broke silence:
'Here I must leave you. May the Lord Almighty
afford His grace in your undertakings
and bring you to safety. Back at the sea-shore
I resume the watch against sea-raiders.'

There was stone paving on the path that brought
the war-band on its way. The war-coats shone
and the links of hard hand-locked iron
sang in their harness as they stepped along
in their gear of grim aspect, going to the hall.
Sea-wearied, they then set against the wall
their broad shields of special temper,
and bowed to bench, battle-shirts clinking,
the war-dress of warriors. The weapons of the seamen
stood in the spear-rack, stacked together,
an ash-wood grey-tipped. These iron-shirted men
were handsomely armed.

                  A high-mannered chieftain
then inquired after the ancestry of the warriors.
'From whence do you bring these embellished shields,
grey mail-shirts, masked helmets,
this stack of spears? I am spokesman here,
herald to Hrothgar; I have not seen
a body of strangers bear themselves more proudly.
It is not exile but adventure, I am thinking,
boldness of spirit, that brings you to Hrothgar.'

The gallant Geat gave answer then,
valour-renowned, and vaunting spoke,
hard under helmet: 'At Hygelac's table

we are sharers in the banquet; Beowulf is my name.
I shall gladly set out to the son of Healfdene,
most famous of kings, the cause of my journey,
lay it before your lord, if he will allow us kindly
to greet in person his most gracious self.'

Then Wulfgar spoke; the warlike spirit
of this Wendel prince, his wisdom in judgement,
were known to many. 'The Master of the Danes,
Lord of the Scyldings, shall learn of your request.
I shall gladly ask my honoured chief,
giver of arm-bands, about your undertaking,
and soon bear the answer back again to you
that my gracious lord shall think good to make.'

He strode rapidly to the seat of Hrothgar,
old and grey-haired among the guard of earls,
stepped forward briskly, stood before the shoulders
of the King of the Danes; a court's ways were known to him.
Then Wulfgar addressed his dear master:
'Men have come here from the country of the Geats,
borne from afar over the back of the sea;
these battle-companions call the man
who leads them, Beowulf. The boon they ask
is, my lord, that they may hold
converse with you. Do not, kind Hrothgar,
refuse them audience in the answer you vouchsafe;
accoutrement would clearly bespeak them
of earls' rank. Indeed the leader
who guided them here seems of great account.'

The Guardian of the Scyldings gave his answer:
'I knew him when he was a child!
It was to his old father, Edgetheow, that
Hrethel the Geat gave in marriage

his one daughter. Well does the son
now pay this call on a proven ally!

    The seafarers used to say, I remember,
who took our gifts to the Geat people
in token of friendship – that this fighting man
in his hand's grasp had the strength
of thirty other men. I am thinking that
the Holy God, as a grace to us
Danes in the West, has directed him here
against Grendel's oppression. This good man shall be
offered treasures in return for his courage.

    Waste no time now but tell them to come in
that they may see this company seated together;
make sure to say that they are most welcome
to the people of the Danes.'
                    Promptly Wulfgar
turned to the doors and told his message:
'The Master of Battles bids me announce,
the Lord of the North Danes, that he knows your ancestry;
I am to tell you all, determined venturers
over the seas, that you are sure of welcome.
You may go in now in your gear of battle,
set eyes on Hrothgar, helmed as you are.
But battle-shafts and shields of linden wood
may here await your words' outcome.'

The prince arose, around him warriors
in dense escort; detailed by the chief,
a group remained to guard the weapons.
The Geats swung in behind their stout leader
over Heorot's floor. The hero led on,
hard under helmet, to the hearth, where he stopped.

Then Beowulf spoke; bent by smith's skill
the meshed rings of his mailshirt glittered.
'Health to Hrothgar! I am Hygelac's kinsman
and serve in his fellowship. Fame-winning deeds
have come early to my hands. The affair of Grendel
has been made known to me on my native turf.
The sailors speak of this splendid hall,
this most stately building, standing idle
and silent of voices, as soon as the evening light
has hidden below the heaven's bright edge.
Whereupon it was urged by the ablest men
among our people, men proved in counsel,
that I should seek you out, most sovereign Hrothgar.
These men knew well the weight of my hands.
Had they not seen me come home from fights
where I had bound five Giants – their blood was upon me –
cleaned out a nest of them? Had I not crushed on the wave
sea-serpents by night in narrow struggle,
broken the beasts? (The bane of the Geats,
they had asked for their trouble.) And shall *I* not try
a single match with this monster Grendel,
a trial against this troll?

               To you I will now
put one request, Royal Scylding,
Shield of the South Danes, one sole favour
that you'll not deny me, dear lord of your people,
now that I have come thus far, Fastness of Warriors;
that I alone may be allowed, with my loyal and determined
crew of companions, to cleanse your hall Heorot.

    As I am informed that this unlovely one
is careless enough to carry no weapon,
so that my lord Hygelac, my leader in war,
may take joy in me, I abjure utterly

the bearing of sword or shielding yellow
board in this battle! With bare hands shall I
grapple with the fiend, fight to the death here,
hater and hated! He who is chosen
shall deliver himself to the Lord's judgement.

If he can contrive it, we may count upon Grendel
to eat quite fearlessly the flesh of Geats
here in this war-hall; has he not chewed
on the strength of this nation? There will be no need, Sir,
for you to bury my head; he will have me gladly,
if death should take me, though darkened with blood.
He will bear my bloody corpse away, bent on eating it,
make his meal alone, without misgiving,
bespatter his moor-lair. The disposing of my body
need occupy you no further then.
But if the fight should take me, you would forward to
      Hygelac
this best of battle-shirts, that my breast now wears.
The queen of war-coats, it is the bequest of Hrethel
and from the forge of Wayland. Fate will take its course!'

Then Hrothgar spoke, the Helmet of the Scyldings:
'So it is to fight in our defence, my friend Beowulf,
and as an office of kindness that you have come to us here!
Great was the feud that your father set off
when his hand struck down Heatholaf in death
among the Wylfings. The Weather-Geats
did not dare to keep him then, for dread of war,
and he left them to seek out the South-Danish folk,
the glorious Scyldings, across the shock of waters.
I had assumed sway over the Scylding nation
and in my youth ruled this rich kingdom,
storehouse of heroes. Heorogar was then dead,
the son of Healfdene had hastened from us,

my elder brother; a better man than I!
I then settled the feud with fitting payment,
sent to the Wylfings over the water's back
old things of beauty; against which I'd the oath of your father.

It is a sorrow in spirit for me to say to any man
– a grief in my heart – what the hatred of Grendel
has brought me to in Heorot, what humiliation,
what harrowing pain. My hall-companions,
my war-band, are dwindled; Weird has swept them
into the power of Grendel. Yet God could easily
check the ravages of this reckless fiend!
They often boasted, when the beer was drunk,
and called out over the ale-cup, my captains in battle,
that they would here await, in this wassailing-place,
with deadliness of iron edges, the onset of Grendel.
When morning brought the bright daylight
this mead-hall was seen all stained with blood:
blood had soaked its shining floor,
it was a house of slaughter. More slender grew my
strength of dear warriors; death took them off. . . .
Yet sit now to the banquet, where you may soon attend,
should the mood so take you, some tale of victory.'

A bench was then cleared for the company of Geats
there in the beer-hall, for the whole band together.
The stout-hearted warriors went to their places,
bore their strength proudly. Prompt in his office,
the man who held the horn of bright mead
poured out its sweetness. The song of the poet
again rang in Heorot. The heroes laughed loud
in the great gathering of the Geats and the Danes.

Then *Unferth* spoke, the son of Edgelaf,
sitting at the feet of the Father of the Scyldings,

unbound a battle-rune. Beowulf's undertaking,
the seaman's bold venture, vexed him much.
He could not allow that another man
should hold under heaven a higher title
to wonders in the world than went with his own name.
'Is this the Beowulf of Breca's swimming-match,
who strove against him on the stretched ocean,
when for pride the pair of you proved the seas
and for a trite boast entrusted your lives
to the deep waters, undissuadable
by effort of friend or foe whatsoever
from that swimming on the sea? A sorry contest!
Your arms embraced the ocean's streams,
you beat the wave-way, wove your hand-movements,
and danced on the Spear-Man. The sea boiled with whelming
waves of winter; in the water's power
you laboured seven nights: and then you *lost* your
     swimming-match,
his might was the greater; morning found him
cast by the sea on the coast of the Battle-Reams.
He made his way back to the marches of the Brondings,
to his father-land, friend to his people,
and to the city-fastness where he had subjects, treasure
and his own stronghold. The son of Beanstan
performed to the letter what he had promised to you.
I see little hope then of a happier outcome
– though in other conflicts elsewhere in the world
you may indeed have prospered – if you propose awaiting
Grendel all night, on his own ground, unarmed.'

Then spoke Beowulf, son of Edgetheow:
'I thank my friend Unferth, who unlocks us this tale
of Breca's bragged exploit; the beer lends
eloquence to his tongue. But the truth is as I've said:

I had more sea-strength, outstaying Breca's,
and endured underwater a much worse struggle.

It was in early manhood that we undertook
with a public boast – both of us still
very young men – to venture our lives
on the open ocean; which we accordingly did.
Hard in our right hands we held each a sword
as we went through the sea, so to keep off
the whales from us. If he whitened the ocean,
no wider appeared the water between us.
He could not away from me; nor would I from him.
Thus stroke for stroke we stitched the ocean
five nights and days, drawn apart then
by cold storm on the cauldron of waters:
under lowering night the northern wind
fell on us in warspite: the waves were rough!

The unfriendliness was then aroused of the fishes of
the deep.
Against sea-beasts my body-armour,
hand-linked and hammered, helped me then,
this forge-knit battleshirt bright with gold,
decking my breast. Down to the bottom
I was plucked in rage by this reptile-fish,
pinned in his grip. But I got the chance
to thrust once at the ugly creature
with my weapon's point: war took off then
the mighty monster; mine was the hand did it.
Then loathsome snouts snickered by me,
swarmed at my throat. I served them out
with my good sword, gave them what they asked for:
those scaly flesh-eaters sat not down
to dine on Beowulf, they browsed not on me
in that picnic they'd designed in the dingles of the sea.

Daylight found them dispersed instead
up along the beaches where my blade had laid them
soundly asleep; since then they have never
troubled the passage of travellers over
that deep water-way. Day in the east grew,
God's bright beacon, and the billows sank
so that I then could see the headlands,
the windy cliffs. "Weird saves oft
the man undoomed if he undaunted be!" –
and it was my part then to put to the sword
seven sea-monsters, in the severest fight
by night I have heard of under heaven's vault;
a man more sorely pressed the seas never held.
I came with my life from the compass of my foes,
but tired from the struggle. The tide bore me
away on its currents to the coasts of the Lapps,
whelms of water.

           No whisper has yet reached me
of sword-ambushes survived, nor such scathing perils
in connection with your name! Never has Breca,
nor you Unferth either, in open battle-play
framed such a deed of daring with your
shining swords – small as my action was.
You have killed only kindred, kept your blade
for those closest in blood; you're a clever man, Unferth,
but you'll endure hell's damnation for that.

    It speaks for itself, my son of Edgelaf,
that Grendel had never grown such a terror,
this demon had never dealt your lord
such havoc in Heorot, had your heart's intention
been so grim for battle as you give us to believe.
He's learnt there's in fact not the least need
excessively to respect the spite of this people,

the scathing steel-thresh of the Scylding nation.
He spares not a single sprig of your Danes
in extorting his tribute, but treats himself proud,
butchering and dispatching, and expects no resistance
from the spear-wielding Scyldings.
                                    I'll show him Geatish
strength and stubbornness shortly enough now,
a lesson in war. He who wishes shall go then
blithe to the banquet when the breaking light
of another day shall dawn for men
and the sun shine glorious in the southern sky.'

Great then was the hope of the grey-locked Hrothgar,
warrior, giver of rings. Great was the trust
of the Shield of the Danes, shepherd of the people,
attending to Beowulf's determined resolve.

There was laughter of heroes, harp-music ran,
words were warm-hearted. *Wealhtheow* moved,
mindful of courtesies, the queen of Hrothgar,
glittering to greet the Geats in the hall,
peerless lady; but to the land's guardian
she offered first the flowing cup,
bade him be blithe at the beer-drinking,
gracious to his people; gladly the conqueror
partook of the banquet, tasted the hall-cup.
The Helming princess then passed about among
the old and the young men in each part of the hall,
bringing the treasure-cup, until the time came
when the flashing-armed queen, complete in all virtues,
carried out to Beowulf the brimming vessel;
she greeted the Geat, and gave thanks to the Lord
in words wisely chosen, her wish being granted
to meet with a man who might be counted on
for aid against these troubles. He took then the cup,

a man violent in war, at Wealhtheow's hand,
and framed his utterance, eager for the conflict.

Thus spoke Beowulf son of Edgetheow:
'This was my determination in taking to the ocean,
benched in the ship among my band of fellows,
that I should once and for all accomplish the wishes
of your adopted people, or pass to the slaughter,
viced in my foe's grip. This vow I shall accomplish,
a deed worthy of an earl; decided otherwise
here in this mead-hall to meet my ending-day!'

This speech sounded sweet to the lady,
the vaunt of the Geat; glittering she moved
to her lord's side, splendid folk-queen.

Then at last Heorot heard once more
words of courage, the carousing of a people
singing their victories; till the son of Healfdene
desired at length to leave the feast,
be away to his night's rest; aware of the monster
brooding his attack on the tall-gabled hall
from the time they had seen the sun's lightness
to the time when darkness drowns everything
and under its shadow-cover shapes do glide
dark beneath the clouds. The company came to its feet.

Then did the heroes, Hrothgar and Beowulf,
salute each other; success he wished him,
control of the wine-hall, and with this word left him:
'Never since I took up targe and sword
have I at any instance to any man beside,
thus handed over Heorot, as I here do to you.
Have and hold now the house of the Danes!
Bend your mind and your body to this task
and wake against the foe! There'll be no want of liberality

71

if you come out alive from this ordeal of courage.'
Then Hrothgar departed, the Protector of the Danes
passed from the hall at the head of his troop.
The war-leader sought Wealhtheow his queen,
the companion of his bed.

              Thus did the King of Glory,
to oppose this Grendel, appoint a hall-guard
– so the tale went abroad – who took on a special
task at the court – to cope with the monster.
The Geat prince placed all his trust
in his mighty strength, his Maker's favour.

He now uncased himself of his coat of mail,
unhelmed his head, handed his attendant
his embellished sword, best of weapons,
and bade him take care of these trappings of war.
Beowulf then made a boasting speech,
the Geat man, before mounting his bed:
'I fancy my fighting-strength, my performance in combat,
at least as greatly as Grendel does his;
and therefore I shall not cut short his life
with a slashing sword – too simple a business.
He has not the art to answer me in kind,
hew at my shield, shrewd though he be
at his nasty catches. No, we'll at night play
without any weapons – if unweaponed he dare
to face me in fight. The Father in His wisdom
shall apportion the honours then, the All-holy Lord,
to whichever side shall seem to Him fit.'

Then the hero lay down, leant his head
on the bolster there; about him many
brave sea-warriors bowed to their hall-rest.
Not one of them thought he would thence be departing
ever to set eyes on his own country,
the home that nourished him, or its noble people;

for they had heard how many men of the Danes
death had dragged from that drinking-hall.
But God was to grant to the Geat people
the clue to war-success in the web of fate –
His help and support; so that they all did
overcome the foe – through the force of one
unweaponed man. The Almighty Lord
has ruled the affairs of the race of men
thus from the beginning.

                    Gliding through the shadows came
the walker in the night; the warriors slept
whose task was to hold the horned building,
all except one. It was well-known to men
that the demon could not drag them to the shades
without God's willing it; yet the one man kept
unblinking watch. He awaited, heart swelling
with anger against his foe, the ordeal of battle.
Down off the moorlands' misting fells came
Grendel stalking; God's brand was on him.
The spoiler meant to snatch away
from the high hall some of human race.
He came on under the clouds, clearly saw at last
the gold-hall of men, the mead-drinking place
nailed with gold plates. That was not the first visit
he had paid to the hall of Hrothgar the Dane:
he never before and never after
harder luck nor hall-guards found.

Walking to the hall came this warlike creature
condemned to agony. The door gave way,
toughened with iron, at the touch of those hands.
Rage-inflamed, wreckage-bent, he ripped open
the jaws of the hall. Hastening on,
the foe then stepped onto the unstained floor,
angrily advanced: out of his eyes stood

an unlovely light like that of fire.
He saw then in the hall a host of young soldiers,
a company of kinsmen caught away in sleep,
a whole warrior-band. In his heart he laughed then,
horrible monster, his hopes swelling
to a gluttonous meal. He meant to wrench
the life from each body that lay in the place
before night was done. It was not to be;
he was no longer to feast on the flesh of mankind
after that night.

        Narrowly the powerful
kinsman of Hygelac kept watch how the ravager
set to work with his sudden catches;
nor did the monster mean to hang back.
As a first step he set his hands on
a sleeping soldier, savagely tore at him,
gnashed at his bone-joints, bolted huge gobbets,
sucked at his veins, and had soon eaten
all of the dead man, even down to his
hands and feet.

        Forward he stepped,
stretched out his hands to seize the warrior
calmly at rest there, reached out for him with his
unfriendly fingers: but the faster man
forestalling, sat up, sent back his arm.
The upholder of evils at once knew
he had not met, on middle earth's
extremest acres, with any man
of harder hand-grip: his heart panicked.
He was quit of the place no more quickly for that.

Eager to be away, he ailed for his darkness
and the company of devils; the dealings he had there
were like nothing he had come across in his lifetime.

Then Hygelac's brave kinsman called to mind
that evening's utterance, upright he stood,
fastened his hold till fingers were bursting.
The monster strained away: the man stepped closer.
The monster's desire was for darkness between them,
direction regardless, to get out and run
for his fen-bordered lair; he felt his grip's strength
crushed by his enemy. It was an ill journey
the rough marauder had made to Heorot.

The crash in the banqueting-hall came to the Danes,
the men of the guard that remained in the building,
with the taste of death. The deepening rage
of the claimants to Heorot caused it to resound.
It was indeed wonderful that the wine-supper-hall
withstood the wrestling pair, that the world's palace
fell not to the ground. But it was girt firmly,
both inside and out, by iron braces
of skilled manufacture. Many a figured
gold-worked wine-bench, as we heard it,
started from the floor at the struggles of that pair.
The men of the Danes had not imagined that
any of mankind by what method soever
might undo that intricate, antlered hall,
sunder it by strength – unless it were swallowed up in
the embraces of fire.
                        Fear entered into
the listening North Danes, as that noise rose up again
strange and strident. It shrilled terror
to the ears that heard it through the hall's side-wall,
the grisly plaint of God's enemy,
his song of ill-success, the sobs of the damned one
bewailing his pain. He was pinioned there

by the man of all mankind living
in this world's estate the strongest of his hands.

Not for anything would the earls' guardian
let his deadly guest go living:
he did not count his continued existence
of the least use to anyone. The earls ran
to defend the person of their famous prince;
they drew their ancestral swords to bring
what aid they could to their captain, Beowulf.
They were ignorant of this, when they entered the fight,
boldly-intentioned battle-friends,
to hew at Grendel, hunt his life
on every side – that no sword on earth,
not the truest steel, could touch their assailant;
for by a spell he had dispossessed all
blades of their bite on him.

                      A bitter parting
from life was that day destined for him;
the eldritch spirit was sent off on his
far faring into the fiends' domain.

It was then that this monster, who, moved by spite
against human kind, had caused so much harm
– so feuding with God – found at last
that flesh and bone were to fail him in the end;
for Hygelac's great-hearted kinsman
had him by the hand; and hateful to each
was the breath of the other.

                    A breach in the giant
flesh-frame showed then, shoulder-muscles
sprang apart, there was a snapping of tendons,
bone-locks burst. To Beowulf the glory
of this fight was granted; Grendel's lot
to flee the slopes fen-ward with flagging heart,

to a den where he knew there could be no relief,
no refuge for a life at its very last stage,
whose surrender-day had dawned. The Danish hopes
in this fatal fight had found their answer.

He had cleansed Heorot. He who had come from afar,
deep-minded, strong-hearted, had saved the hall
from persecution. He was pleased with his night's work,
the deed he had done. Before the Danish people
the Geat captain had made good his boast,
had taken away all their unhappiness,
the evil menace under which they had lived,
enduring it by dire constraint,
no slight affliction. As a signal to all
the hero hung up the hand, the arm
and torn-off shoulder, the entire limb,
Grendel's whole grip, below the gable of the roof.

There was, as I heard it, at hall next morning
a great gathering in the gift-hall yard
to see the wonder. Along the wide highroads
the chiefs of the clans came from near and far
to see the foe's footprints. It may fairly be said
that his parting from life aroused no pity in any
who tracked the spoor-blood of his blind flight
for the monster's mere-pool; with mood flagging
and strength crushed, he had staggered onwards;
each step evidenced his ebbing life's blood.

The tarn was troubled; a terrible wave-thrash
brimmed it, bubbling; black-mingled,
the warm wound-blood welled upwards.
He had dived to his doom, he had died miserably;
here in his fen-lair he had laid aside
his heathen soul. Hell welcomed it.

Then the older retainers turned back on the way
journeyed with much joy; joined by the young men,
the warriors on white horses wheeled away from the mere
in bold mood. Beowulf's feat
was much spoken of, and many said,
that between the seas, south or north,
over earth's stretch no other man
beneath the sky's shifting excelled Beowulf,
of all who wielded the sword he was worthiest to rule.
In saying this they did not slight in the least
the gracious Hrothgar, for he was a good king.

Where, as they went, their way broadened
they would match their mounts, making them leap
along the best stretches, the strife-eager
on their fallow horses. Or a fellow of the king's,
whose head was a storehouse of the storied verse,
whose tongue gave gold to the language
of the treasured repertory, wrought a new lay
made in the measure. The man struck up,
found the phrase, framed rightly
the deed of Beowulf, drove the tale,
rang word-changes.
                    Of Wæls's great son,
Sigemund, he spoke then, spelling out to them
all he had heard of that hero's strife,
his fights, strange feats, far wanderings,
the feuds and the blood spilt. Fitela alone heard
these things not well nor widely known to men,
when Sigemund chose to speak in this vein
to his sister's son. They were inseparable
in every fight, the firmest of allies;
their swords had between them scythed to the ground
a whole race of monsters. The reputation

that spread at his death was no slight one:
Sigemund it was who had slain the dragon,
the keeper of the hoard; the king's son walked
under the grey rock, he risked alone
that fearful conflict; Fitela was not there.
Yet it turned out well for him, his weapon transfixed
the marvellous snake, struck in the cave-wall,
best of swords; the serpent was dead.
Sigemund's valour had so prevailed
that the whole ring-hoard was his to enjoy
dispose of as he wished. Wæls's great son
loaded his ship with shining trophies,
stacking them by the mast; the monster shrivelled away.

He was by far the most famous of adventurers
among the peoples, this protector of warriors,
for the deeds by which he had distinguished himself.
Heremod's stature and strength had decayed then,
his daring diminished. Deeply betrayed
into the fiends' power, far among the Giants
he was dispatched to death. Dark sorrows
drove him mad at last. A deadly grief
he had become to his people and the princes of his land.
Wise men among the leaders had lamented that career,
their fierce one's fall, who in former days
had looked to him for relief of their ills,
hoping that their lord's son would live and in ripeness
assume the kingdom, the care of his people,
the hoard and the stronghold, the storehouse of heroes,
the Scylding homeland. Whereas Hygelac's kinsman
endeared himself ever more deeply to friends
and to all mankind, evil seized Heremod.

The riders returning came racing their horses
along dusty-pale roads. The dawn had grown

into broadest day, and, drawn by their eagerness
to see the strange sight, there had assembled at the hall
many keen warriors. The king himself,
esteemed for excellence, stepped glorious
from his wife's chambers, the warden of ring-hoards,
with much company; and his queen walked
the mead-path by him, her maidens following.

Taking his stand on the steps of the hall,
Hrothgar beheld the hand of Grendel
below the gold gable-end; and gave speech:
'Let swift thanks be given to the Governor of All,
seeing this sight! I have suffered a thousand
spites from Grendel: but God works ever
miracle upon miracle, the Master of Heaven.
Until yesterday I doubted whether
our afflictions would find a remedy
in my lifetime, since this loveliest of halls
stood slaughter-painted, spattered with blood.
For all my counsellors this was a cruel sorrow,
for none of them imagined they could mount a defence
of the Scylding stronghold against such enemies,
warlocks, demons!

             But one man has,
by the Lord's power, performed the thing
that all our thought and arts to this day
had failed to do. She may indeed say,
whoever she be that brought into the world
this young man here – if yet she lives –
that the God of Old was gracious to her
in her child-bearing. Beowulf, I now take you
to my bosom as a son, O best of men,
and cherish you in my heart. Hold yourself well
in this new relation! You will lack for nothing

that lies in my gift of the goods of this world:
lesser offices have elicited reward,
we have honoured from our hoard less heroic men,
far weaker in war. But you have well ensured
by the deeds of your hands an undying honour
for your name for ever. May the Almighty Father
yield you always the success that you yesternight enjoyed!'

Beowulf spoke, son of Edgetheow:
'We willingly undertook this test of courage,
risked a match with the might of the stranger,
and performed it all. I would prefer, though,
that you had rather seen the rest of him here,
the whole length of him, lying here dead.
I had meant to catch him, clamp him down
with a cruel lock to his last resting-place;
with my hands upon him, I would have him soon
in the throes of death – unless he disappeared!
But I had not a good enough grip to prevent
his getting away, when God did not wish it;
the fiend in his flight was far too violent,
my life's enemy. But he left his hand
behind him here, so as to have his life,
and his arm and shoulder. And all for nothing:
it bought him no respite, wretched creature.
He lives no longer, laden with sins,
to plague mankind: pain has set
heavy hands on him, and hasped about him
fatal fetters. He is forced to await now,
like a guilty criminal, a greater judgement,
where the Lord in His splendour shall pass sentence upon
    him.'

The son of Edgelaf was more silent then
in boasting of his own battle-deeds:

the athelings gazed at what the earl's strength
had hung there – the hand, high up under the roof,
and the fingers of their foe. From the front, each one
of the nail-sockets seemed steel to the eye,
each spur on the hand of that heathen warrior
was a terrible talon. They told each other
nothing could be hard enough to harm it at all,
not the most ancient of iron swords
would bite on that bloody battle-hand.

Other hands were then pressed to prepare the inside
of the banqueting-hall, and briskly too.
Many were ready, both men and women,
to adorn the guest-hall. Gold-embroidered tapestries
glowed from the walls, with wonderful sights
for every creature that cared to look at them.
The bright building had badly started
in all its inner parts, despite its iron bands,
and the hinges were ripped off. Only the roof survived
unmarred and in one piece when the monstrous one,
flecked with his crimes, had fled the place
in despair of his life.
                              But to elude death
is not easy: attempt it who will,
he shall go to the place prepared for each
of the sons of men, the soul-bearers
dwelling on earth, ordained them by fate:
laid fast in that bed, the body shall sleep
when the feast is done.
                              In due season
the king himself came to the hall;
Healfdene's son would sit at the banquet.
No people has gathered in greater retinue,
borne themselves better about their ring-giver.

82

Men known for their courage came to the benches,
rejoiced in the feast; they refreshed themselves kindly
with many a mead-cup; in their midst the brave kinsmen,
father's brother and brother's son,
Hrothgar and Hrothulf. Heorot's floor was
filled with friends: falsity in those days
had no place in the dealings of the Danish people.

Then as a sign of victory the son of Healfdene
bestowed on Beowulf a standard worked in gold,
a figured battle-banner, breast and head-armour;
and many admired the marvellous sword
that was borne before the hero. Beowulf drank with
the company in the hall. He had no cause to be ashamed of
gifts so fine before the fighting-men!
I have not heard that many men at arms
have given four such gifts of treasure
more openly to another at the mead.
At the crown of the helmet, the head-protector,
was a rim, with wire wound round it, to stop
the file-hardened blade that fights have tempered
from shattering it, when the shield-warrior
must go out against grim enemies.

The king then ordered eight war-horses
with glancing bridles to be brought within walls
and onto the floor. Fretted with gold
and studded with stones was one saddle there!
This was the battle-seat of the Bulwark of the Danes,
when in the sword-play the son of Healfdene
would take his part; the prowess of the king
had never failed at the front where the fighting was mortal.
The Protector of the Sons of Scyld then gave
both to Beowulf, bidding him take care
to use them well, both weapons and horses.

Thus did the glorious prince, guardian of the treasure,
reward these deeds, with both war-horses and armour;
of such open-handedness no honest man
could ever speak in disparagement.

Then the lord of men also made a gift
of treasure to each who had adventured with Beowulf
over the sea's paths, seated now at the benches –
an old thing of beauty. He bade compensation
to be made too, in gold, for the man whom Grendel
had horribly murdered; more would have gone
had not the God overseeing us, and the resolve of a man,
stood against this Weird. The Wielder guided then
the dealings of mankind, as He does even now.
A mind that seeks to understand and grasp this
is therefore best. Both bad and good,
and much of both, must be borne in a lifetime
spent on this earth in these anxious days.

Then string and song sounded together
before Healfdene's Helper-in-battle:
the lute was taken up and tales recited
when Hrothgar's bard was bidden to sing
a hall-song for the men on the mead-benches.
It was how disaster came to the sons of *Finn*:
first the Half-Dane champion, *Hnæf* of the Scyldings,
was fated to fall in the Frisian ambush.
Hildeburgh their lady had little cause to speak
of the good faith of the Jutes; guiltless she had suffered
in that linden-wood clash the loss of her closest ones,
her son and her brother, both born to die there,
struck down by the spear. Sorrowful princess!
This decree of fate the daughter of Hoc
mourned with good reason; for when morning came
the clearness of heaven disclosed to her

the murder of those kindred who were the cause of all
her earthly bliss.
                    Battle had also claimed
all but a few of Finn's retainers
in that place of assembly; he was unable therefore
to bring to a finish the fight with *Hengest*,
force out and crush the few survivors
of Hnæf's troop. The truce-terms they put to him
were that he should make over a mead-hall to the Danes,
with high-seat and floor; half of it
to be held by them, half by the Jutes.
In sharing out goods, that the son of Folcwalda
should every day give honour to the Danes
of Hengest's party, providing rings
and prizes from the hoard, plated with gold,
treating them identically in the drinking-hall
as when he chose to cheer his own Frisians.
On both sides they then bound themselves fast
in a pact of friendship. Finn then swore
strong unexceptioned oaths to Hengest
to hold in honour, as advised by his counsellors,
the battle-survivors; similarly no man
by word or deed to undo the pact,
as by mischievous cunning to make complaint of it,
despite that they were serving the slayer of their prince,
since their lordless state so constrained them to do;
but that if any Frisian should fetch the feud to mind
and by taunting words awaken the bad blood,
it should be for the sword's edge to settle it then.

The pyre was erected, the ruddy gold
brought from the hoard, and the best warrior
of Scylding race was ready for the burning.
Displayed on his pyre, plain to see

were the bloody mail-shirt, the boars on the helmets,
iron-hard, gold-clad; and gallant men about him
all marred by their wounds; mighty men had fallen there.
Hildeburgh then ordered her own son
to be given to the funeral fire of Hnæf
for the burning of his bones; bade him be laid
at his uncle's side. She sang the dirges,
bewailed her grief. The warrior went up;
the greatest of corpse-fires coiled to the sky,
roared before the mounds. There were melting heads
and bursting wounds, as the blood sprang out
from weapon-bitten bodies. Blazing fire,
most insatiable of spirits, swallowed the remains
of the victims of both nations. Their valour was no more.

The warriors then scattered and went to their homes.
Missing their comrades, they made for Friesland,
the home and high stronghold. But Hengest still,
as he was constrained to do, stayed with Finn
a death-darkened winter in dreams of his homeland.
He was prevented from passage of the sea
in his ring-beaked boat: the boiling ocean
fought with the wind; winter locked the seas
in his icy binding; until another year
came at last to the dwellings, as it does still,
continually keeping its season,
the weather of rainbows.
                              Now winter had fled
and earth's breast was fair, the exile strained
to leave these lodgings; yet it was less the voyage
that exercised his mind than the means of his vengeance,
the bringing about of the bitter conflict
that he meditated for the men of the Jutes.
So he did not decline the accustomed remedy,

when the son of Hunlaf set across his knees
that best of blades, his battle-gleaming sword;
the Giants were acquainted with the edges of that steel.

And so, in his hall, at the hands of his enemies,
Finn received the fatal sword-thrust;
Guthlaf and Oslaf, after the sea-crossing,
proclaimed their tribulations, their treacherous entertainment,
and named the author of them; anger in the breast
rose irresistible. Red was the hall then
with the lives of foemen. Finn was slain there,
the king among his troop, and the queen taken.
The Scylding crewmen carried to the ship
the hall-furnishings of Friesland's king,
all they could find at Finnsburgh
in gemstones and jewelwork. Journeying back,
they returned to the Danes their true-born lady,
restored her to her people.

                    Thus the story was sung,
the gleeman's lay. Gladness mounted,
bench-mirth rang out, the bearers gave
wine from wonderful vessels. Then came Wealhtheow
   forward,
going with golden crown to where the great heroes
were sitting, uncle and nephew; their bond was sound at
   that time,
each was true to the other. Likewise Unferth the spokesman
sat at the footstool of Hrothgar. All had faith in his spirit,
accounted his courage great – though toward his kinsmen
   he had not been
kind at the clash of swords.

                  The Scylding queen then spoke:

'Accept this cup, my king and lord,

giver of treasure. Let your gaiety be shown,
gold-friend of warriors, and to the Geats speak
in words of friendship, for this well becomes a man.
Be gracious to these Geats, and let the gifts you have had
from near and far, not be forgotten now.

     I hear it is your wish to hold this warrior
henceforward as your son. Heorot is cleansed,
the ring-hall bright again: therefore bestow while you may
these blessings liberally, and leave to your kinsmen
the land and its people when your passing is decreed,
your meeting with fate. For may I not count
on my gracious Hrothulf to guard honourably
our young ones here, if you, my lord,
should give over this world earlier than he?
I am sure that he will show to our children
answerable kindness, if he keeps in remembrance
all that we have done to indulge and advance him,
the honours we bestowed on him when he was still a child.'

Then she turned to the bench where her boys were sitting,
Hrethric and Hrothmund, among the heroes' sons,
young men together; where the good man sat also
between the two brothers, Beowulf the Geat.
Then the cup was taken to him and he was entreated kindly
to honour their feast; ornate gold
was presented in trophy: two arm-wreaths,
with robes and rings also, and the richest collar
I have ever heard of in all the world.

Never under heaven have I heard of a finer
prize among heroes – since Hama carried off
the Brising necklace to his bright city,
that gold-cased jewel; he gave the slip

to the machinations of Eormenric, and made his name
  forever.

This gold was to be on the neck of the grandson of
  Swerting
on the last of his harryings, Hygelac the Geat,
as he stood before the standard astride his plunder,
defending his war-haul: Weird struck him down;
in his superb pride he provoked disaster
in the Frisian feud. This fabled collar
the great war-king wore when he crossed
the foaming waters; he fell beneath his shield.
The king's person passed into Frankish hands,
together with his corselet, and this collar also.
They were lesser men that looted the slain;
for when the carnage was over, the corpse-field was littered
with the people of the Geats.
                        Applause filled the hall;
then Wealhtheow spoke, and her words were attended.

'Take pride in this jewel, have joy of this mantle
drawn from our treasuries, most dear Beowulf!
May fortune come with them and may you flourish in your
  youth!
Proclaim your strength; but in counsel to these boys
be a gentle guardian, and my gratitude will be seen.
Already you have so managed that men everywhere
will hold you in honour for all time,
even to the cliffs at the world's end, washed by Ocean,
the wind's range. All the rest of your life
must be happy, prince; and prosperity I wish you too,
abundance of treasure! But be to my son
a friend in deed, most favoured of men.
You see how open is each earl here with his neighbour,
temperate of heart, and true to his lord.

The nobles are loyal, the lesser people dutiful;
wine mellows the men to move to my bidding.'

She walked back to her place. What a banquet that was!
The men drank their wine: the weird they did not know,
destined from of old, the doom that was to fall
on many of the earls there. When evening came
Hrothgar departed to his private bower,
the king to his couch; countless were the men
who watched over the hall, as they had often done before.
They cleared away the benches, and covered the floor
with beds and bolsters: the best at the feast
bent to his hall-rest, hurried to his doom.
Each by his head placed his polished shield,
the lindens of battle. On the benches aloft,
above each atheling, easily to be seen,
were the ring-stitched mail-coat, the mighty helmet
steepling above the fray, and the stout spear-shaft.
It was their habit always, at home or on campaign,
to be ready for war, in whichever case,
whatsoever the hour might be
that the need came on their lord: what a nation they were!

Then they sank into sleep. A savage penalty
one paid for his night's rest! It was no new thing for that
   people
since Grendel had settled in the gold-giving hall,
working his evil, until the end came,
death for his misdeeds. It was declared then to men,
and received by every ear, that for all this time
a survivor had been living, an avenger for their foe
and his grim life's-leaving: *Grendel's Mother* herself,
a monstrous ogress, was ailing for her loss.
She had been doomed to dwell in the dread waters,
in the chilling currents, because of that blow

whereby Cain became the killer of his brother,
his own father's son. He stole away, branded,
marked for his murder, from all that men delight in,
to inhabit the wastelands.
                              Hosts of the ill ones
sprang from his begetting; as Grendel, that hateful
accursed outcast, who encountered at Heorot
a watchful man, waiting for the fight.
The grim one fastened his grip upon him there,
but he remembered his mighty strength,
the gift that the Lord had so largely bestowed on him,
and, putting his faith in the favour of the Almighty
and His aid and comfort, he overcame the foe,
put down the hell-fiend. How humbling was that flight
when the miserable outcast crept to his dying-place!
Thus mankind's enemy. But his Mother now purposed
to set out at last – savage in her grief –
on that wrath-bearing visit of vengeance for her son.

She came down to Heorot, where the heroes of the Danes
slept about the hall. A sudden change
was that for the men there when the Mother of Grendel
found her way in among them – though the fury of her
   onslaught
was less frightful than his; as the force of a woman,
her onset in a fight, is less feared by men,
where the bound blade, beaten out by hammers,
cuts, with its sharp edges shining with blood,
through the boars that bristle above the foes' helmets!

Many a hard sword was snatched up in the hall
from its rack above the benches; the broad shield was raised,
held in the hand firm; helmet and corselet
lay there unheeded when the horror was on them.
She was all eager to be out of the place

now that she was discovered, and escape with her life.
She caught a man quickly, clutched him to herself,
one of the athelings, and was away to the fen.
This was the hero that Hrothgar loved better
than any on earth among his retinue,
destroyed thus as he slept; he was a strong warrior,
noted in battle. (Beowulf was not there:
separate lodging had been assigned that night,
after the treasure-giving, to the Geat champion.)
Heorot was in uproar; the hand had gone with her,
blood-stained, familiar.
                              And so a fresh sorrow
came again to those dwellings. It was an evil bargain,
with both parties compelled to barter
the lives of their dearest. What disturbance of spirit
for the wise king, the white-haired soldier,
hearing the news that the nearest of his thanes
was dead and gone, his dearest man!

Beowulf was soon summoned to the chamber,
victory-blest man. And that valiant warrior
came with his following – it was at first light –
captain of his company, to where the king waited
to see if by some means the Swayer of All
would work a turning into this tale of sorrow.
The man excellent in warfare walked across the hall
flanked by his escort – the floor-timbers boomed –
to make his addresses to the Danish lord,
the Guide of the Ingwine. He inquired of him whether
the night had been quiet, after a call so urgent.

Hrothgar spoke, the Helmet of the Scyldings:
'Do not ask about our welfare! Woe has returned
to the Danish people with the death of *Ashhere*,
the elder brother of Yrmenlaf.

He was my closest counsellor, he was keeper of my thoughts,
he stood at my shoulder when we struck for our lives
at the crashing together of companies of foot,
when blows rained on boar-crests. Men of birth and merit
all should be as Ashhere was!
A bloodthirsty monster has murdered him in Heorot,
a wandering demon; whither this terrible one,
glorying in her prey, glad of her meal,
has returned to, I know not. She has taken vengeance
for the previous night, when you put an end to Grendel
with forceful finger-grasp, and in a fierce manner,
because he had diminished and destroyed my people
for far too long. He fell in that struggle
and forfeited his life; but now is followed by another
most powerful ravager. Revenge is her motive,
and in furthering her son's feud she has gone far enough,
– or thanes may be found who will think it so;
in their breasts they will grieve for their giver of rings,
bitter at heart. For the hand is stilled
that would openly have granted your every desire.

   I have heard it said by subjects of mine
who live in the country, counsellors in this hall,
that they have seen such a pair
of huge wayfarers haunting the moors,
otherworldly ones; and one of them,
so far as they might make it out,
was in woman's shape; but the shape of a man,
though twisted, trod also the tracks of exile
– save that he was more huge than any human being.
The country people have called him from of old
by the name of Grendel; they know of no father for
   him,
nor whether there have been such beings before

among the monster-race.
                              Mysterious is the region
they live in – of wolf-fells, wind-picked moors
and treacherous fen-paths: a torrent of water
pours down dark cliffs and plunges into the earth,
an underground flood. It is not far from here,
in terms of miles, that the Mere lies,
overcast with dark, crag-rooted trees
that hang in groves hoary with frost.
An uncanny sight may be seen at night there
– the fire in the water! The wit of living men
is not enough to know its bottom.
The hart that roams the heath, when hounds have pressed
   him
long and hard, may hide in the forest
his antlered head; but the hart will die there
sooner than swim and save his life;
he will sell it on the brink there, for it is not a safe place.
And the wind can stir up wicked storms there,
whipping the swirling waters up
till they climb the clouds and clog the air,
making the skies weep.
                              Our sole remedy
is to turn again to you. The treacherous country
where that creature of sin is to be sought out
is strange to you as yet: seek then if you dare!
I shall reward the deed, as I did before,
with wealthy gifts of wreathèd ore,
treasures from the hoard, if you return again.'

Beowulf spoke, son of Edgetheow:
'Bear your grief, wise one! It is better for a man
to avenge his friend than to refresh his sorrow.
As we must all expect to leave

our life on this earth, we must earn some renown,
if we can, before death; daring is the thing
for a fighting man to be remembered by.

Let Denmark's lord arise, and we shall rapidly see then
where this kinswoman of Grendel's has gone away to!
I can promise you this, that she'll not protect herself by
    hiding
in any fold of the field, in any forest of the mountain,
in any dingle of the sea, dive where she will!
For this day, therefore, endure all your woes
with the patience that I may expect of you.'

The ancient arose and offered thanks to God,
to the Lord Almighty, for what this man had spoken.
A steed with braided mane was bridled then,
a horse for Hrothgar; the hero-patriarch
rode out shining; shieldbearers marched
in troop beside him. The trace of her going
on the woodland paths was plainly to be seen,
stepping onwards; straight across
the fog-bound moor she had fetched away there
the lifeless body of the best man
of all who kept the courts of Hrothgar.
The sons of men then made their way
up steep screes, by scant tracks
where only one might walk, by wall-faced cliffs,
through haunted fens – uninhabitable country.

Going on ahead with a handful of the
keener men to reconnoitre,
Beowulf suddenly saw where some ash-trees
hung above a hoary rock
– a cheerless wood! And the water beneath it
was turbid with blood; bitter distress

was to be endured by the Danes who were there,
a grief for the earls, for every thane
of the Friends of the Scyldings, when they found there
the head of Ashhere by the edge of the cliff.

The men beheld the blood on the water,
its warm upwellings. The war-horn sang
an eager battle-cry. The band of foot-soldiers,
sitting by the water, could see multitudes
of strange sea-drakes swerving through the depths,
and water-snakes lay on the ledges of the cliffs,
such serpents and wild beasts as will sally out
in middle morning to make havoc
in the seas where ships sail.
                              Slithering away
at the bright phrases of the battle-horn,
they were swollen with anger. An arrow from the
bow of Beowulf broke the life's thread
of one wave-thrasher; wedged in his throat
the iron dart; with difficulty then
did he swim through the deep, until death took him.
They struck him as he swam, and straightaway,
with their boar-spears barbed and tanged;
gaffed and battered, he was brought to the cliff-top,
strange lurker of the waves. They looked with wonder
at their grisly guest!
                        The Geat put on
the armour of a hero, unanxious for his life:
the manufacture of the mailed shirt,
figured and vast, that must venture in the deep,
made it such a bulwark to his bone-framed chest
that the savage attack of an incensed enemy
could do no harm to the heart within it.
His head was encircled by a silver helmet

that was to strike down through the swirl of water,
disturb the depths. Adorned with treasure,
clasped with royal bands, it was right as at first
when the weapon-smith had wonderfully made it,
so that no sword should afterward be able to cut through
the defending wild boars that faced about it.
Not least among these mighty aids
was the hilted sword that Hrothgar's spokesman,
Unferth, lent him in his hour of trial.
Hrunting was its name; unique and ancient,
its edge was iron, annealed in venom
and tempered in blood; in battle it never
failed any hero whose hand took it up
at his setting out on a stern adventure
for the house of foes. This was not the first time
that it had to do heroic work.

It would seem that the strapping son of Edgelaf
had forgotten the speech he had spoken earlier,
eloquent with wine, for he offered the weapon now
to the better swordsman; himself he would not go
beneath the spume to display his valour
and risk his life; he lost his reputation there
for nerve and action. With the other man
it was otherwise once he had armed himself for battle.

Beowulf spoke, son of Edgetheow:
'I am eager to begin, great son of Healfdene.
Remember well, then, my wise lord,
provider of gold, what we agreed once before,
that if in your serivce it should so happen
that I am sundered from life, that you would assume the
   place
of a father towards me when I was gone.
Now extend your protection to the troop of my companions,

my young fellows, if the fight should take me;
convey also the gifts that you have granted to me,
beloved Hrothgar, to my lord Hygelac.
For on seeing this gold, the Geat chieftain,
Hrethel's son, will perceive from its value
that I had met with magnificent patronage
from a giver of jewels and that I had joy of him.
Let Unferth have the blade that I inherited
– he is a widely-known man – this wave-patterned sword
of rare hardness. With Hrunting shall I
achieve this deed – or death shall take me!'

After these words the Weather-Geat prince
dived into the Mere – he did not care
to wait for an answer – and the waves closed over
the daring man. It was a day's space almost
before he could glimpse ground at the bottom.

The grim and greedy guardian of the flood,
keeping her hungry hundred-season watch,
discovered at once that one from above,
a human, had sounded the home of the monsters.
She felt for the man and fastened upon him
her terrible hooks; but no harm came thereby
to the hale body within – the harness so ringed him
that she could not drive her dire fingers
through the mesh of the mail-shirt masking his limbs.

When she came to the bottom she bore him to her lair,
the mere-wolf, pinioning the mail-clad prince.
Not all his courage could enable him
to draw his sword; but swarming through the water,
throngs of sea-beasts threw themselves upon him
with ripping tusks to tear his battle-coat,
tormenting monsters. Then the man found

that he was in some enemy hall
where there was no water to weigh upon him
and the power of the flood could not pluck him away,
sheltered by its roof: a shining light he saw,
a bright fire blazing clearly.

It was then that he saw the size of this water-hag,
damned thing of the deep. He dashed out his weapon,
not stinting the stroke, and with such strength and violence
that the circled sword screamed on her head
a strident battle-song. But the stranger saw
his battle-flame refuse to bite
or hurt her at all; the edge failed
its lord in his need. It had lived through many
hand-to-hand conflicts, and carved through the helmets
of fated men. This was the first time
that this rare treasure had betrayed its name.
Determined still, intent on fame,
the nephew of Hygelac renewed his courage.
Furious, the warrior flung it to the ground,
spiral-patterned, precious in its clasps,
stiff and steel-edged; his own strength would suffice him,
the might of his hands. A man must act so
when he means in a fight to frame himself
a long-lasting glory; it is not life he thinks of.

The Geat prince went for Grendel's mother,
seized her by the shoulder – he was not sorry to be fighting –
his mortal foe, and with mounting anger
the man hard in battle hurled her to the ground.
She promptly repaid this present of his
as her ruthless hands reached out for him;
and the strongest of fighting-men stumbled in his weariness,
the firmest of foot-warriors fell to the earth.
She was down on this guest of hers and had drawn her knife,

broad, burnished of edge; for her boy was to be avenged,
her only son. Overspreading his back,
the shirt of mail shielded his life then,
barred the entry to edge and point.
Edgetheow's son would have ended his venture
deep under ground there, the Geat fighter,
had not the battle-shirt then brought him aid,
his war-shirt of steel. And the wise Lord,
the holy God, gave out the victory;
the Ruler of the Heavens rightly settled it
as soon as the Geat regained his feet.

He saw among the armour there the sword to bring him
    victory,
a Giant-sword from former days: formidable were its edges,
a warrior's admiration. This wonder of its kind
was yet so enormous that no other man
would be equal to bearing it in battle-play
– it was a Giant's forge that had fashioned it so well.
The Scylding champion, shaking with war-rage,
caught it by its rich hilt, and, careless of his life,
brandished its circles, and brought it down in fury
to take her full and fairly across the neck,
breaking the bones; the blade sheared
through the death-doomed flesh. She fell to the ground;
the sword was gory; he was glad at the deed.

Light glowed out and illumined the chamber
with a clearness such as the candle of heaven
sheds in the sky. He scoured the dwelling
in single-minded anger, the servant of Hygelac;
with his weapon high, and, holding to it firmly,
he stalked by the wall. Nor was the steel useless yet
to that man of battle, for he meant soon enough
to settle with Grendel for those stealthy raids

– there had been many of them – he had made on the
   West-Danes;
far more often than on that first occasion
when he had killed Hrothgar's hearth-companions,
slew them as they slept, and in their sleep ate up
of the folk of Denmark fifteen good men,
carrying off another of them
in foul robbery. The fierce champion
now settled this up with him: he saw where Grendel
lay at rest, limp from the fight;
his life had wasted through the wound he had got
in the battle at Heorot. The body gaped open
as it now suffered the stroke after death
from the hard-swung sword; he had severed the neck.

And above, the wise men who watched with Hrothgar
the depths of the pool descried soon enough
blood rising in the broken water
and marbling the surface. Seasoned warriors,
grey-headed, experienced, they spoke together,
said it seemed unlikely that they would see once more
the prince returning triumphant to seek out
their famous master. Many were persuaded
the she-wolf of the deep had done away with him.
The ninth hour had come; the keen-hearted Scyldings
abandoned the cliff-head; the kindly gold-giver
turned his face homeward. But the foreigners sat on,
staring at the pool with sickness at heart,
hoping they would look again on their beloved captain,
believing they would not.
                      The blood it had shed
made the sword dwindle into deadly icicles;
the war-tool wasted away. It was wonderful indeed
how it melted away entirely, as the ice does in the spring

when the Father unfastens the frost's grip,
unwinds the water's rope – He who watches over
the times and the seasons; He is the true God.

The Geat champion did not choose to take
any treasures from that hall, from the heaps he saw there,
other than that richly ornamented hilt,
and the head of Grendel. The engraved blade
had melted and burnt away: the blood was too hot,
the fiend that had died there too deadly by far.
The survivor of his enemies' onslaught in battle
now set to swimming, and struck up through the water;
both the deep reaches and the rough wave-swirl
were thoroughly cleansed, now the creature from the
   otherworld
drew breath no longer in this brief world's space.

Then the seamen's Helm came swimming up
strongly to land, delighting in his sea-trove,
those mighty burdens that he bore along with him.
They went to meet him, a manly company,
thanking God, glad of their lord,
seeing him safe and sound once more.
Quickly the champion's corselet and helmet
were loosened from him. The lake's waters,
sullied with blood, slept beneath the sky.

Then they turned away from there and retraced their steps,
pacing the familiar paths back again
as bold as kings, carefree at heart.
The carrying of the head from the cliff by the Mere
was no easy task for any of them,
brave as they were. They bore it up,
four of them, on a spear, and transported back
Grendel's head to the gold-giving hall.

Warrior-like they went, and it was not long
before they came, the fourteen bold Geats,
marching to the hall, and, among the company
walking across the land, their lord the tallest.
The earl of those thanes then entered boldly
– a man who had dared deeds and was adorned with their
    glory,
a man of prowess – to present himself to Hrothgar.
Then was the head of Grendel, held up by its locks,
manhandled in where men were drinking;
it was an ugly thing for the earls and their queen,
an awesome sight; they eyed it well.

Beowulf spoke, son of Edgetheow:
'Behold! What you see here, O son of Healfdene,
prince of the Scyldings, was pleasant freight for us:
– these trophies from the lake betoken victory!

     Not easily did I survive
the fight under water; I performed this deed
not without a struggle. Our strife had ended
at its very beginning if God had not saved me.
Nothing could I perform in that fight with Hrunting,
it had no effect, fine weapon though it be.
But the Guide of mankind granted me the sight
– He often brings aid to the friendless –
of a huge Giant-sword hanging on the wall,
ancient and shining – and I snatched up the weapon.
When the hour afforded, in that fight I slew
the keepers of the hall. The coiling-patterned
blade burnt all away, as the blood sprang forth,
the hottest ever shed; the hilt I took from them.
So I avenged the violent slaughter
and outrages against the Danes; indeed it was fitting.
Now, I say, you may sleep in Heorot

free from care – your company of warriors
and every man of your entire people,
both the young men and the guard. Gone is the need
to fear those fell attacks of former times
on the lives of your earls, my lord of the Scyldings.'

Then the golden hilt was given into the hand
of the older warrior, the white-haired leader.
A Giant had forged it. With the fall of the demons
it passed into the possession of the prince of the Danes,
this work of wonder-smiths. The world was rid
of that invidious enemy of God
and his mother also, with their murders upon them;
and the hilt now belonged to the best of the kings
who ruled the earth in all the North
and distributed treasure between the seas.
Hrothgar looked on that long-treasured hilt
before he spoke. The spring was cut on it
of the primal strife, with the destruction at last
of the race of Giants by the rushing Flood,
a terrible end. Estranged was that race
from the Lord of Eternity: the tide of water
was the final reward that the Ruler sent them.
On clear gold labels let into the cross-piece
it was rightly told in runic letters,
set down and sealed, for whose sake it was
that the sword was first forged, that finest of iron,
spiral-hilted, serpent-bladed.
                              At the speaking of the wise
son of Healfdene the hall was silent:
'He who has long tendered justice and truth to his people,
their shepherd from of old, surely may say this,
remembering all that's gone – that this man was born
to be the best of men. Beowulf, my friend,

your name shall resound in the nations of the earth
that are furthest away.

                       How wise you are to bear
your great strength so peaceably! I shall perform my vows
agreed in our forewords. It is granted to your people
that you shall live to be a long-standing comfort
and bulwark to the heroes.

                       Heremod was not so
for the honoured Scyldings, the sons of Edgewela:
his manhood brought not pleasure but a plague upon us,
death and destruction to the Danish tribes.
In his fits he would cut down his comrade in war
and his table-companion – until he turned away
from the feastings of men, that famous prince.
This though the Almighty had exalted him in the bliss
of strength and vigour, advancing him far
above all other men. Yet inwardly his heart-hoard
grew raw and blood-thirsty; no rings did he give
to the Danes for his honour. And he dwelt an outcast,
paid the penalty for his persecution of them
by a life of sorrow. Learn from this, Beowulf:
study openhandedness! It is for your ears that I relate this,
and I am old in winters.

                       It is wonderful to recount
how in his magnanimity the Almighty God
deals out wisdom, dominion and lordship
among mankind. The Master of all things
will sometimes allow to the soul of a man
of well-known kindred to wander in delight:
He will grant him earth's bliss in his own homeland,
the sway of the fortress-city of his people,
and will give him to rule regions of the world,
wide kingdoms: he cannot imagine,
in his unwisdom, that an end will come.

His life of bounty is not blighted by hint
of age or ailment; no evil care
darkens his mind, malice nowhere
bares the sword-edge, but sweetly the world
swings to his will; worse is not looked for.
At last his part of pride within him
waxes and climbs, the watchman of the soul
slumbering the while. That sleep is too deep,
tangled in its cares! Too close is the slayer
who shoots the wicked shaft from his bow!
For all his armour he is unable to protect himself:
the insidious bolt buries in his chest,
the crooked counsels of the accursed one.
What he has so long enjoyed he rejects as too little;
in niggardly anger renounces his lordly
gifts of gilt torques, forgets and misprises
his fore-ordained part, endowed thus by God,
the Master of Glory, with these great bounties.
And ultimately the end must come,
the frail house of flesh must crumble
and fall at its hour. Another then takes
the earl's inheritance; open-handedly
he gives out its treasure, regardless of fear.

Beloved Beowulf, best of warriors,
resist this deadly taint, take what is better,
your lasting profit. Put away arrogance,
noble fighter! The noon of your strength
shall last for a while now, but in a little time
sickness or a sword will strip it from you:
either enfolding flame or a flood's billow
or a knife-stab or the stoop of a spear
or the ugliness of age; or your eyes' brightness

lessens and grows dim. Death shall soon
have beaten you then, O brave warrior!

    So it is with myself. I swayed the Ring-Danes
for fifty years here, defending them in war
with ash and with edge over the earth's breadth
against many nations; until I numbered at last
not a single adversary beneath the skies' expanse.
But what change of fortune befell me at my hearth
with the coming of Grendel; grief sprang from joy
when the old enemy entered our hall!
Great was the pain that persecution
thrust upon me. Thanks be to God,
the Lord everlasting, that I have lived until this day,
seen out this age of ancient strife
and set my gaze upon this gory head!
But join those who are seated, and rejoice in the feast,
O man clad in victory! We shall divide between us
many treasures when morning comes.'

The Geat went most gladly to take
his seat at the bench, at the bidding of the wise one.
Quite as before, the famous men,
guests of the hall, were handsomely feasted
on this new occasion. Then night's darkness
grew on the company. The guard arose,
for their wise leader wished to rest,
the grey-haired Scylding. The Geat was ready enough
to go to his bed too, brave shieldsman.

The bower-thane soon brought on his way
this fight-wearied and far-born man.
His courteous office was to care for all
a guest's necessities, such as at that day
the wants of a seafaring warrior might be.

The hero took his rest; the hall towered up
gilded, wide-gabled, its guest within sleeping
until the black raven blithe-hearted greeted
the heaven's gladness. Hastening, the sunlight
shook out above the shadows. Sharp were the bold ones,
each atheling eager to set off,
back to his homeland: the high-mettled stranger
wished to be forging far in his ship.
That hardy man ordered Hrunting to be carried
back to the son of Edgelaf, bade him accept again
his well-loved sword; said that he accounted it
formidable in the fight, a good friend in war,
thanked him for the loan of it, without the least finding
    fault
with the edge of that blade; ample was his spirit!

By then the fighting-men were fairly armed-up
and ready for the journey; the Joy of the Danes went,
a prince, to the high seat where Hrothgar was,
one hero brave in battle hailed the other.

Beowulf then spoke, son of Edgetheow.
'We now wish to say, seafarers who
are come from far, how keenly we desire
to return again to Hygelac. Here we were rightly,
royally, treated; you have entertained us well.
If I can ever on this earth earn of you,
O lord of men, more of your love
than I have so far done, by deeds of war,
I shall at once be ready. If ever I hear
that the neighbouring tribes intend your harm,
as those who hate you have done in the past,
I'll bring a thousand thanes and heroes
here to help you. As for Hygelac, I know
that the Lord of the Geats, Guide of his flock,

young though he is, will yield his support
both in words and deeds so I may do you honour
and bring you a grove of grey-tipped spears
and my strength in aid when you are short of men.
Further, when Hrethric shall have it in mind
to come, as a king's son, to the courts of the Geats
he shall find many friends there. Far countries are seen
to more advantage by a man of valour.'

Hrothgar spoke to him in answer:
'These words you have delivered, the Lord in His wisdom
put in your heart. I have heard no man
of the age that you are utter such wisdom.
You are rich in strength and ripe of mind,
you are wise in your utterance. If ever it should happen
that spear or other spike of battle,
sword or sickness, should sweep away
the son of Hrethel, your sovereign lord,
shepherd of his people, my opinion is clear,
that the Sea-Geats will not be seeking for a better
man to be their king and keep their war-hoard,
if you still have life and would like to rule
the kingdom of your kinsmen. As I come to know
your temper, dear Beowulf, the better it pleases me.
You have brought it about that both the peoples,
the Sea-Geats and the Spear-Danes,
shall share out peace; the shock of war,
the old sourness, shall cease between us.
So long as I shall rule the reaches of this kingdom
we shall exchange wealth; a chief shall greet
his fellow with gifts over the gannet's bath
as the ship with curved prow crosses the seas
with presents and pledges. Your people, I know,

always open-natured in the old manner,
are fast to friends and firm toward enemies.'

Then the Shield of the Heroes, Healfdene's son,
presented him with twelve new treasures in the hall,
bade him with these tokens betake himself
safe to his people; and soon return again.
Then that king of noble race, ruler of the Scyldings,
embraced and kissed that best of thanes,
taking him by the neck; tears fell from
the grey-haired one. With the wisdom of age
he foresaw two things, the second more likely,
that they would never again greet one another,
meet thus as heroes. The man was so dear to him
that he could not stop the surging in his breast;
but hidden in the heart, held fast in its strings,
a deep longing for this dearly loved man
burned against the blood.

                                   Beowulf went from him,
trod the green earth, a gold-resplendent warrior
rejoicing in his rings. Riding at anchor
the strayer of ocean stayed for her master.
Chiefly the talk returned as they walked
to Hrothgar's giving. He was a king
blameless in all things, until old age at last,
that brings down so many, removed his proud strength.

They came then to the sea-flood, the spirited band
of warrior youth, wearing the ring-meshed
coat of mail. The coastguard saw
the heroes approaching, as he had done before.
Nor was it ungraciously that he greeted the strangers
from his ridge by the cliff, but rode down to meet them:
how welcome they would be to the Weather-Geats, he said
to those shipward-bound men in their shining armour.

The wide sea-boat with its soaring prow
was loaded at the beach there with battle-raiment,
with horses and arms. High rose the mast
above the lord Hrothgar's hoard of gifts.
To the boat-guard Beowulf gave
a gold-cleated sword; it gained the man
much honour on the mead-benches,
that treasured heirloom. Out moved the boat then
to divide the deep water, left Denmark behind.
A special sea-dress, a sail, was hoisted
and belayed to the mast. The beams spoke.
The wind did not hinder the wave-skimming ship
as it ran through the seas, but the sea-going craft
with foam at its throat, furled back the waves,
her ring-bound prow planing the waters
till they caught sight of the cliffs of the Geats
and headlands they knew. The hull drove ahead,
urged by the breeze, and beached on the shore.

The harbour-guard was waiting at the water's edge;
his eye had been scouring the stretches of the flood
in a long look-out for these loved men.
Now he moored the broad-ribbed boat in the sand,
held fast with hawsers, so no heft of the waves
should drive away again those darling timbers.
He had the heroes' hoard brought ashore,
their gold-plated armour. To go to their lord
was now but a step, to see again Hygelac
the son of Hrethel, at his home where he dwells
himself with his hero-band, hard by the sea-wall.

That was a handsome hall there. And high within it sat
a king of great courage. His consort was young,
but wise and discreet for one who had lived
so few years at court; the queen's name was *Hygd*,

Hareth's daughter. When she dealt out treasure
to the Geat nation, the gifts were generous,
there was nothing narrowly done.

                      It was not so with that other
proud young queen, who was cruel to her people.
There was no one so rash among the retainers of the house
as to risk a look at her – except her lord himself –
turn his eyes on her, even by day;
or fatal bonds were fettled for him,
twisted by hand: and when hands had been laid on him
he could be sure that the sword would be present,
and settle it quickly, its spreading inlays
proclaim its killing-power. Unqueenly ways
for a woman to follow, that one who weaves peace,
though of matchless looks, should demand the life
of a well-loved man for an imagined wrong!
Hemming's son *Offa* put an end to that.
And the ale-drinkers then told a tale quite different:
little was the hurt or harm that she brought
on her subjects then, as soon as she was given,
gold-decked, in marriage, to the mighty young champion
of valiant lineage, when she voyaged out
on the gleaming flood at her father's bidding
to the hall of Offa. All that followed
of a life destined to adorn a throne
she employed well, and was well-loved for it,
strong in her love for that leader of heroes,
the outstanding man, as I have heard tell,
of all mankind's mighty race
from sea to sea. So it was that Offa,
brave with the spear, was spoken of abroad
for his wars and his gifts; he governed with wisdom
the land of his birth. To him was born Eomer,

helper of the heroes, Hemming's kinsman,
Garmund's grandson, great in combat.

The war-man himself came walking along
by the broad foreshores with his band of picked men,
trod the sea-beach. From the south blazed
the sun, the world's candle. They carried themselves forward,
stepping on eagerly to the stronghold where
Ongentheow's conqueror, the earls' defender,
the warlike young king, was well-known for his
giving of neck-rings. The news of Beowulf's
return was rapidly told to Hygelac
– that the shield of the warriors, his own shoulder-companion,
had walked alive within the gates,
unscathed from the combat, and was coming to the hall.
The floor was quickly cleared of men
for the incoming guests, by order of the king.

When he had offered greetings in grave words,
as usage obliged him, to his lord of men,
the survivor of the fight sat facing the king,
kinsman and kinsman. Carrying the mead-cup
about the hall was Hareth's daughter,
lover of the people, presenting the wine-bowl
to the hand of each Geat. Hygelac then made
of his near companion in that noble hall
courteous inquiry. Curiosity burned in him
to hear the adventures of this voyage of the Geats.

'What luck did you meet with, beloved Beowulf,
on your suddenly resolved seeking out
of distant strife over salt water,
battle at Heorot? Did you bring to that famous
leader Hrothgar some alleviation
of those woes so widely known? Overwhelming doubts

troubled my mind, mistrusting this voyage
of my dear liegeman. Long did I beg you
never to meet with this murderous creature
but to let the South Danes themselves bring an end
to their feud with Grendel. God be thanked
that safe and sound I see you here today!'

Thus spoke Beowulf, son of Edgetheow:
'It has been told aloud, my lord Hygelac,
and to many men by now, the meeting that there was
between myself and Grendel, the great time
we fought in that place where he had inflicted so much
grief and outrage, age-long disgrace
on the Victor-Scyldings. I avenged all.
No kinsman of Grendel shall have cause to take pride
in the sound that arose in the stretches of the night
– not the last of that alien and evil brood
on the face of the earth.
                    First I went in
to greet Hrothgar in the hall of the ring-giving.
As soon as the glorious son of Healfdene
knew my mind, he immediately
offered me a seat at his sons' bench.
What hall-joys were there! A happier company
seated over mead I've not met with in my time
beneath the heavens. A noble princess
fit to be the pledge of peace between nations
would move among the younger men in the hall,
stirring their spirits; she would bestow a torque
often upon a warrior before she went to her seat.
Or the heroes would look on as Hrothgar's daughter
bore the ale-flagon to each earl in turn.
I heard those who sat in the hall calling her

by the name of *Freawaru* as she fetched each warrior
the nailed treasure-cup.

                    She is betrothed to *Ingeld*,
this girl attired in gold, to the gracious son of Froda.
The Protector of the Danes has determined this
and accounts it wisdom, the keeper of the land,
thus to end all the feud and their fatal wars
by means of the lady. Yet when a lord is dead
it is seldom the slaying-spear sleeps for long –
seldom indeed – dear though the bride may be.

    The lord of the Heathobards may not like it well
at the bringing home of his bride to the hall:
nor may it please every earl in that nation
to have the pride and daring of Denmark at table
– their guests resplendent in the spoil of their ancestors!
Heathobards had treasured these trenchant, ring-patterned
weapons until they could wield them no longer
– until they took part in that play of the shields,
destroyed themselves and their dear companions.

    An old spear-fighter shall speak at the feast,
eyeing the hilt-ring – his heart grows fierce
as he remembers all the slaying of the men by the spear.
In his dark mood he deliberately
tries out the mettle of a man who is younger,
awakens his war-taste; such words he utters:
"My friend, is that not a familiar sword?
Your father carried it forth to battle,
– excellent metal – masked as for war
on his last expedition. There the Danes slew him,
the keen Scyldings, and kept the field
when Withergyld was dead, when the warriors had fallen.
The son of one of his slayers now
sports the weapon here, and, spurning our hall-floor,

boasts of the killing: he carries at his side
the prize that you should possess by right."

      With such biting words of rebuke and reminder
he taunts him at every turn; until the time comes
when one sleeps blood-stained from the blow of a sword:
the follower of the lady forfeits with his life
for the actions of his father; the other contrives
to lose himself, and lives; the land is familiar to him.
Both sides then will break the pact
sworn by the earls; and Ingeld's vengefulness
will well up in him, overwhelming gall
shall cause his wife-love to cool thereafter.
So I do not believe that this liking of the Heathobards
for alliance with the Danes is all what it seems,
or that their friendship is sound.

                        I shall speak further
of Grendel again, O giver of treasure,
that you may rightly know the result of the champions'
hand-to-hand meeting. When heaven's jewel
had glided from the world, the wrathful creature,
dire dusk-fiend, came down to seek us out
where, still whole, we held the building.
The weight of the fight fell on Handscio,
the doomed blow came down on him; he died the first,
a warrior in his harness; the hero, my fellow,
was ground to death between Grendel's jaws,
our friend's body was bolted down whole.
But the bloody-toothed slayer, bent on destruction,
was not going to go from that gold-giving hall
any the sooner: not empty-handed!
Proud of his might, he made proof of me,
groped out his greedy palm. A glove hung from it,
uncouth and huge, clasped strangely,

and curiously contrived; it was cobbled together
all of dragons' skins, and with devilish skill.
It was inside this bag that the bold marauder
was going to put me, guiltless as I was,
as the first of his catch; but he could not manage it
once I had stood up in anger against him.
Too long to repeat here how I paid back
the enemy of the people for his every crime;
but to your people, O my prince, my performance there
will bring honour. He broke away,
tasted life's joys for a little while,
but his strong right hand stayed behind
in the hall of Heorot; humbled he went thence
and sank despairing in the depths of the Mere.

    For this deadly fight the Friend of the Scyldings
recompensed me with plated gold,
a mort of treasure, when the morrow came
and we had benched ourselves at the banqueting table.
There was music and laughter, lays were sung:
the veteran of the Scyldings, versed in the sagas,
would himself fetch back far-off times to us;
the daring-in-battle would address the harp,
the joy-wood, delighting; or deliver a reckoning
both true and sad; or he would tell us the story
of some wonderful adventure, valiant-hearted king.
Or the seasoned warrior, wrapped in age,
would again fall to fabling of his youth
and the days of his battle-strength; his breast was troubled
as his mind filled with the memories of those years.

    And thus we spent the space of a day there
seeking delight, until the ensuing dusk
came to mankind. Quick on its heels
the mother of Grendel moved to her revenge,

spurred on by sorrow; her son was death-taken
by Geat warspite. That gruesome she
avenged her son, struck down a warrior,
and boldly enough! The breath was taken
from the ancient counsellor, Ashhere, there.
Nor could the Danish people, when day came,
give their death-wearied dear one to be burned,
escort him to the pyre: she had carried the body
to the mountain-torrent's depth in her monstrous embrace.
This was for Hrothgar the harshest of the blows
that since so long had fallen on the leader of the people.
Distraught with care, the king then asked of me
a noble action – and in your name, Hygelac –
that I should risk my life among the rush of waters
and perform a great deed; he promised me reward.

   Far and wide it is told how I found in the surges
the grim and terrible guardian of the deep.
After a hard hand-to-hand struggle
the whirlpool boiled with the blood of the mother;
I had hewn off her head in that hall underground
with a sword of huge size. I survived that fight
not without difficulty; but my doom was not yet.

   The protector of warriors rewarded me
with a heap of treasure, Healfdene's son.
The ways of that king accorded to usage:
I was not to forgo the guerdon he had offered,
the meed of my strength; he bestowed upon me
the treasures I would have desired, the son of Healfdene;
now, O bravest of kings, I bring them to you.
I rejoice to present them. Joy, for me, always
lies in your gift. Little family
do I have in the world, Hygelac, besides yourself.'

Then he bade them bring in the boar's head standard,
the battle-dwarfing helmet, the hoar war-shirt
and the lambent sword; and delivered this speech:
'Hrothgar gave me all this garb of war
with one word – the wisest of princes –
that I should first relate to you whose legacy it is.
His brother Heorogar had it, he told me,
for a long while, as Lord of the Scyldings,
yet chose not to give this guardian of his breast
to his own son, the spirited Heoroweard,
friend though he was to him.

                    Flourish in the use of it!'

I heard that four fast-stepping horses
followed these treasures, a team of bays
matching as apples. All these he gave him,
both horses and armour – the act of a kinsman!
A kinsman knits no nets of malice
darkly for his fellow. Does he devise the end
of the man that is next to him? The nephew of Hygelac
held fast to that man hardy in battle;
each thought only of the other's welfare.

I heard that he presented Hygd with a neck-ring,
the wonderful treasure-work Wealhtheow had given him
– high was her breeding – and three horses also,
graceful in their gait, and with gay saddles.
Her breast was made more beautiful by the jewel.

Such was the showing of the son of Edgetheow,
known for his combats and his courage in action.
His dealings were honourable: in drink he did not strike
at the slaves of his hearth; his heart was not savage.
The hero guarded well the great endowment
God had bestowed on him, a strength unequalled

among mankind. He had been misprised for long,
the sons of the Geats seeing little in him
and the lord of the Weather-Geats not willing to pay him
much in the way of honour on the mead-benches.
They firmly believed in his laziness
–'the atheling was idle'! But for all such humblings
time brought reversal, invested him with glory.

Then the king bold in war, keeper of the warriors,
required them to bring in the bequest of Hrethel,
elaborate in gold; the Geats at that day
had no more royal treasure of the rank of sword.
This he then laid in the lap of Beowulf
and bestowed on him an estate of seven thousand hides,
a chief's stool and a hall. Inherited land,
a domain by birthright, had come down to them both
in the Geat nation; the greater region
to the better-born of them – the broad kingdom.

But it fell out after, in other days,
among the hurl of battle – when Hygelac lay dead
and the bills of battle had dealt death to his Heardred,
despite the shield's shelter, when the Scylfings found him
amid his conquering people, and those keen war-wolves
grimly hemmed in Hereric's nephew –
that the broad kingdom came by this turn
into Beowulf's hands.
                              Half a century
he ruled it, well: until One began
– the king had grown grey in the guardianship of the land –
to put forth his power in the pitch-black night-times
– the hoard-guarding *Dragon* of a high barrow
raised above the moor.
                         Men did not know
of the way underground to it; but one man did enter,

went right inside, reached the treasure,
the heathen hoard, and his hand fell
on a golden goblet. The guardian, however,
if he had been caught sleeping by the cunning of the thief,
did not conceal this loss. It was not long till the near-
dwelling people discovered that the dragon was angry.

The causer of his pain had not purposed this;
it was without relish that he had robbed the hoard;
necessity drove him. The nameless slave
of one of the warriors, wanting shelter,
on the run from a flogging, had felt his way inside,
a sin-tormented soul. When he saw what was there
the intruder was seized with sudden terror;
but for all his fear, the unfortunate wretch
still took the golden treasure-cup. . . .
There were heaps of hoard-things in this hall underground
which once in gone days gleamed and rang;
the treasure of a race rusting derelict.

In another age an unknown man,
brows bent, had brought and hid here
the beloved hoard. The whole race
death-rapt, and of the ring of earls
one left alive; living on in that place
heavy with friend-loss, the hoard-guard
waited the same weird. His wit acknowledged
that the treasures gathered and guarded over the years
were his for the briefest while.

                      The barrow stood ready
on flat ground where breakers beat at the headland,
new, near at hand, made narrow of access.
The keeper of rings carried into it
the earls' holdings, the hoard-worthy part
fraught with gold, and few words he spoke:

'Hold, ground, the gold of the earls!
Men could not. Cowards they were not
who took it from thee once, but war-death took them,
that stops life, struck them, spared not one
man of my people, passed on now.
They have had their hall-joys. I have not with me
a man able to unsheathe this. . . .
Who shall polish this plated vessel,
this treasured cup? The company is elsewhere.

    This hardened helmet healed with gold
shall lose its shell. They sleep now
whose work was to burnish the battle-masks;
so with the cuirass that in the crash took
bite of iron among breaking shields:
it moulders with the man. This mail-shirt travelled far,
hung from a shoulder that shouldered warriors:
it shall not jingle again.
               There's no joy from harp-play,
glee-wood's gladness, no good hawk
swings through hall now, no swift horse
tramps at the threshold. Terrible slaughter
has carried into darkness many kindreds of mankind.'

So the sole survivor, in sorrowful mood,
bewailed his grief; he wandered cheerless
through days and nights until death's flood
reached to his heart.
           The Ravager of the night,
the burner who has sought out barrows from of old,
then found this hoard of undefended joy.
The smooth evil dragon swims through the gloom
enfolded in flame; the folk of that country
hold him in dread. He is doomed to seek out

hoards in the ground, and guard for an age there
the heathen gold: much good does it do him!

Thus for three hundred winters this waster of peoples
guarded underground the great hoard-hall
with his enormous might; until a man awoke
the anger in his breast by bearing to his master
the plated goblet as a peace-offering,
a token of new fealty. Thus the treasure was lightened
and the treasure-house was breached; the boon was granted
to the luckless slave, and his lord beheld
for the first time that work of a former race of men.

The waking of the worm awoke the feud:
he glided along the rock, glared at the sight
of a foeman's footprint: far too near his head
the intruder had stepped as he stole by him!
(An undoomed man may endure affliction
and even exile lightly, for as long as the Ruler
continues to protect him.) The treasure-guard eagerly
quartered the ground to discover the man
who had done him wrong during his sleep.
Seething with rage, he circled the barrow's
whole outer wall, but no hint of a man
showed in the wilderness. Yet war's prospect pleased him,
the thought of battle-action! He went back into the mound
to search for the goblet, and soon saw that one
of the tribe of men had tampered with the gold
of the glorious hoard.
                              The hoard's guardian
waited until evening only with difficulty.
The barrow-keeper was bursting with rage:
his fire would cruelly requite the loss
of the dear drinking-vessel.

                         At last day was gone,
to the worm's delight; he delayed no further
inside his walls, but issued forth flaming,
armed with fire.
                         That was a fearful beginning
for the people of that country; uncomfortable and swift
was the end to be likewise for their lord and treasure-giver!

So the visitant began to vomit flames
and burn the bright dwellings; the blazing rose skyward
and men were afraid: the flying scourge
did not mean to leave one living thing.
On every side the serpent's ravages,
the spite of the foe, sprang to the eye –
how this hostile assailant hated and injured
the men of the Geats. Before morning's light
he flew back to the hoard in its hidden chamber.
He had poured out fire and flame on the people,
he had put them to the torch; he trusted now to the barrow's
    walls
and to his fighting strength; his faith misled him.

Beowulf was acquainted quickly enough
with the truth of the horror, for his own hall had itself
been swallowed in flame, the finest of buildings,
and the gift-stool of the Geats. Grief then struck
into his ample heart with anguished keenness.
The chieftain supposed he had sorely angered
the Ruler of all, the eternal Lord,
by breach of ancient law. His breast was thronged
with dark unaccustomed care-filled thoughts.
The fiery dragon's flames had blasted
all the land by the sea, and its safe stronghold,
the fortress of the people. The formidable king
of the Geats now planned to punish him for this.

The champion of the fighting-men, chief of the earls,
gave commands for the making of a marvellous shield
worked all in iron; well he knew
that a linden shield would be of little service
– wood against fire. For the foremost of athelings
the term of his days in this transitory world
was soon to be endured; it was the end, too, for the dragon's
long watch over the wealth of the hoard.

The distributor of rings disdained to go
with a troop of men or a mighty host
to seek the far-flier. He had no fear for himself
and discounted the worm's courage and strength,
its prowess in battle. Battles in plenty
he had survived; valiant in all dangers,
he had come through many clashes since his cleansing of
   Heorot
and his extirpation of the tribe of Grendel,
hated race.
            That was hardly the least
of hand-to-hand combats when Hygelac was slain,
when that kindly lord of peoples, the king of the Geats,
the son of Hrethel, among the hurl of battle
slaked the sword's thirst on the soil of Friesland
and the blows beat down on him!
                        Beowulf came away
by the use of his force in a feat of swimming;
alone into the ocean he leapt, holding
thirty men's mail-coats on his arm.

There was little cause for crowing among the Hetware
about their conduct of the foot-fight: they carried their
   lindens
forward against him; but few came back
from the wolf in war, walked home again.

Solitary and wretched was the son of Edgetheow
on the sweep of waters as he swam back to his people.
There Hygd offered him the 'hoard and the kingdom,
the gift-stool and its treasure; not trusting that her son
would be able to hold the inherited seats
against foreign peoples now his father was dead.
But the bereaved people could arrive at no conditions
under which the atheling would accept the kingdom
or allow himself to be lord over Heardred.
Rather he fostered him among the people with friendly
   counsel,
with kindliness and respect, until he came of age
and ruled the Geats.
                  Guests sought out Heardred,
outcasts from overseas: Ohthere's sons.

They had risen against Onela, ruler of the Scylfings,
highest of the princes who provided treasure
in all the sea-coasts of the Swedish realms,
a famous lord. This led to the end
of Hygelac's son; his hospitality
cost him a weapon-thrust and a wound to the life.
Ongentheow's son, Onela, turned
to seek his home again once Heardred was dead;
the gift-stool and the ruling of the Geat people
he left to Beowulf; who was a brave king,
and kept it before his mind to requite his lord's death.
In after-days he was Eadgils' friend
when Eadgils was deserted, supporting his cause
across the wide water with weapons and an army,
Ohthere's son; who took his own revenge
by terror-campaigns that at last trapped Onela.

So the son of Edgetheow survived unscathed
each of these combats, calamitous onslaughts,

works of prowess: until this one day
when he must wage war on the serpent.
The Lord of the Geats went with eleven companions
to set eyes on the dragon; his anger rose in him.
He had by then discovered the cause of the attack
that had ravaged his people; the precious drinking-cup
had passed into his hands from the hands of the finder.
He who had brought about the beginning of the feud
now made the thirteenth man in their company;
a miserable captive; cowed, he must show them
the way to the place, an unwilling guide.
For he alone knew the knoll and its earth-hall,
hard by the strand and the strife of the waves,
the underground hollow heaped to the roof
with intricate treasures. Attendant on the gold
was that underground ancient, eager as a wolf,
an awesome guardian; it was no easy bargain
for any mortal man to make himself its owner.

The stern war-king sat on the headland,
spoke encouragement to the companions of his hearth,
the gold-friend of the Geats. Gloomy was his spirit though,
death-eager, wandering; the weird was at hand
that was to overcome the old man there,
seek his soul's hoard, and separate
the life from the body; not for long now
would the atheling's life be lapped in flesh.

Beowulf spoke, son of Edgetheow:
'Many were the struggles I survived in youth
in times of danger; I do not forget them.
When that open-handed lord beloved by the people
received me from my father I was seven years old:
King Hrethel kept and fostered me,
gave me treasure and table-room, true to our kinship.

All his life he had as little hatred for me,
a warrior in hall, as he had for a son,
Herebeald, or Hathkin, or Hygelac my own lord.

A murderous bed was made for the eldest
by the act of a kinsman, contrary to right:
a shaft from Hathkin's horn-tipped bow
shot down the man that should have become his lord;
mistaking his aim, he struck his kinsman,
his own brother, with the blood-stained arrow-head.
A sin-fraught conflict that could not be settled,
unthinkable in the heart; yet thus it was,
and the atheling lost his life unavenged.

Grief such as this a grey-headed man
might feel if he saw his son in youth
riding the gallows. Let him raise the lament then,
a song of sorrow, while his son hangs there,
a sport for the raven. Remedy is there none
that an age-stricken man may afford him then.
Every morning reminds him again
that his son has gone elsewhere; another son,
an heir in his courts, he cares not to wait for,
now that the first has found his deeds
have come to an end in the constriction of death.
He sorrows to see among his son's dwellings
the wasted wine-hall, the wind's home now,
bereft of all joy. The riders are sleeping,
the heroes in the grave. The harp does not sound,
there is no laughter in the yard as there used to be of old.
He goes then to his couch, keens the lament
for his one son alone there; too large now seem to him
his houses and fields.
                    The Helm of the Geats
sustained a like sorrow for Herebeald

surging in his heart. Hardly could he settle
the feud by imposing a price on the slayer;
no more could he offer actions to that warrior
manifesting hatred; though he held him not dear.

Hard did this affliction fall upon him:
he renounced men's cheer, chose God's light.
But he left to sons his land and stronghold
at his life's faring-forth – as the fortunate man does.

On Hrethel's death the hatred and strife
of the Swedes and the Geats, the grievances between them
broke into bitter war across the broad water.
The sons of Ongentheow were strong fighters,
active in war; they would not keep
peace on the lakes, but plotted many
a treacherous ambush about Hreosnabeorgh.

It has come to be known that my kinsmen and friends
revenged both the feud and the violent attack,
though the price that one of them paid was his life,
a hard bargain. That battle proved
mortal for Hathkin, Master of the Geats.
But came the morrow, and a kinsman, as I heard,
avenged him on his slayer with the sword's edge:
in his attack on Eofor, Ongentheow's
war-mask shattered, and the Scylfing patriarch
fell pale from the wound; the wielding hand
forgot not the feud, flinched not from the death-blow.

I had the fortune in that battle, by my bright sword,
to make return to Hygelac for the treasures he had given
    me.
He had granted me land, land to enjoy
and leave to my heirs. Little need was there
that Hygelac should go to the Gifthas or the Spear-Danes

or seek out ever in the Swedish kingdom
a weaker champion, and chaffer for his services.
I was always before him in the footing host,
by myself in the front.

        So, while I live,
I shall always do battle, while this blade lasts
that early and late has often served me
since, with my bare hands, I broke Dayraven,
the champion of the Franks, before the flower of the host.
He was not to be permitted to present his Frisian lord
with the breast-armour that had adorned Hygelac,
for he was slain in the struggle, the standard-bearer,
noble in his prowess. It was not my sword
that broke his bone-cage and the beatings of his heart
but my warlike hand-grasp.

        Now shall hard edge,
hand and blade, do battle for the hoard!'

Beowulf made speech, spoke a last time
a word of boasting: 'Battles in plenty
I ventured in youth; and I shall venture this feud
and again achieve glory, the guardian of my people,
old though I am, if this evil destroyer
dares to come out of his earthen hall.'

Then he addressed each of the men there
on this last occasion, courageous helm-bearers,
cherished companions: 'I would choose not to take
any weapon to this worm, if I well knew
of some other fashion fitting to my boast
of grappling with this monster, as with Grendel before.
But as I must expect here the hot war-breath
of venom and fire, for this reason I have
my board and corselet. From the keeper of the barrow
I shall not flee one foot; but further than that

shall be worked out at the wall as Weird shall decide for us,
every man's master. My mood is strong;
I forgo further words against the winged fighter.

Men in armour! Your mail-shirts protect you:
await on the barrow the one of us two
who shall be better able to bear his wounds
after this onslaught. This affair is not for you,
nor is it measured to any man but myself alone
to match strength with this monstrous being,
attempt this deed. By daring will I
win this gold; war otherwise
shall take your king, terrible life's-bane!'

The strong champion stood up beside his shield,
brave beneath helmét, he bore his mail-shirt
to the rocky cliff's foot, confident in his strength,
a single man; such is not the coward's way!
Then did the survivor of a score of conflicts,
the battle-clashes of encountering armies,
excelling in manhood, see in the wall
a stone archway, and out of the barrow broke
a stream surging through it, a stream of fire
with waves of deadly flame; the dragon's breath
meant he could not venture into the vault near the hoard
for any time at all without being burnt.

Passion filled the prince of the Geats:
he allowed a cry to utter from his breast,
roared from his stout heart: as the horn clear in battle
his voice re-echoed through the vault of grey stone.
The hoard-guard recognized a human voice,
and there was no more time for talk of friendship:
hatred stirred. Straightaway

the breath of the dragon billowed from the rock
in a hissing gust; the ground boomed.

He swung up his shield, overshadowed by the mound,
the lord of the Geats against this grisly stranger.
The temper of the twisted tangle-thing was fired
to close now in battle. The brave warrior-king
shook out his sword so sharp of edge,
an ancient heirloom. Each of the pair,
intending destruction, felt terror at the other:
intransigent beside his towering shield
the lord of friends, while the fleetness of the serpent
wound itself together; he waited in his armour.
It came flowing forward, flaming and coiling,
rushing on its fate.
                    For the famous prince
the protection lent to his life and person
by the shield was shorter than he had shaped it to be.
He must now dispute this space of time,
the first in his life when fate had not assigned him
the glory of the battle. The Geat chieftain
raised his hand, and reached down such a stroke
with his huge ancestral sword on the horribly-patterned
    snake
that, meeting the bone, its bright edge turned
and it bit less strongly than its sorely-straitened lord
required of it then. The keeper of the barrow
after this stroke grew savage in mood,
spat death-fire; the sparks of their battle
blazed into the distance.
                          He boasted of no triumphs then,
the gold-friend of the Geats, for his good old sword
bared in the battle, his blade, had failed him,
as such iron should not do.

That was no easy adventure,
when the celebrated son of Edgetheow
had to pass from that place on earth
and against his will take up his dwelling
in another place; as every man must give up
the days that are lent him.

It was not long again
to the next meeting of those merciless ones.
The barrow-guard took heart: his breast heaved
with fresh out-breath: fire enclosed
the former folk-king; he felt bitter pain.

The band of picked companions did not come
to stand about him, as battle-usage asks,
offspring of athelings; they escaped to the wood,
saved their lives.

Sorrow filled
the breast of one man. The bonds of kinship
nothing may remove for a man who thinks rightly.
This was *Wiglaf*, Weoxstan's son,
well-loved shieldsman, a Scylfing prince
of the stock of Alfhere; he could see his lord
tormented by the heat through his mask of battle.
He remembered then the favours he had formerly bestowed
    on him,
the wealthy dwelling-place of the Waymundings,
confirming him in the landrights his father had held.
He could not then hold back: hand gripped the yellow
linden-wood shield, shook out that ancient
sword that Eanmund, Ohthere's son,
had left among men.

He met his end in battle,
a friendless exile, felled by the sword
wielded by Weoxstan: who went back to his kinsmen

with the shining helm, the shirt of ring-mail
and the ancient giant-sword. All this war-harness,
eager for use, Onela then gave to him,
though it had been his nephew's; nor did he speak
of the blood-feud to the killer of his brother's son.
Weoxstan kept this war-gear many years,
sword and breast-armour, till his son was able
to perform manly deeds as his father had of old.
He gave him among the Geats these garments of battle
of incalculable worth; then went his life's journey
wise and full of years.
                For the youthful warrior
this was the first occasion when he was called on to stand
at his dear lord's shoulder in the shock of battle.
His courage did not crumble, nor did his kinsman's heirloom
weaken at the war-play: as the worm found out
when they had got to grips with one another.

Wiglaf then spoke many words that were fitting,
addressed his companions; dark was his mood.
'I remember the time, as we were taking mead
in the banqueting hall, when we bound ourselves
to the gracious lord who granted us arms,
that we would make return for these trappings of war,
these helms and hard swords, if an hour such as this
should ever chance for him. He chose us himself
out of all his host for this adventure here,
expecting action; he armed me with you
because he accounted us keen under helmet,
men able with the spear – even though our lord
intended to take on this task of courage
as his own share, as shepherd of the people,
and champion of mankind in the achieving of glory
and deeds of daring.

That day has now come
when he stands in need of the strength of good fighters,
our lord and liege. Let us go to him,
help our leader for as long as it requires,
the fearsome fire-blast. I had far rather
that the flame should enfold my flesh-frame there
alongside my gold-giver – as God knows of me.
To bear our shields back to our homes
would seem unfitting to me, unless first we have been able
to kill the foe and defend the life
of the prince of the Weather-Geats. I well know
that former deeds deserve not that, alone
of the flower of the Geats, he should feel the pain,
sink in the struggle; sword and helmet,
corselet and mail-shirt, shall be our common gear.'

He strode through the blood-smoke, bore his war-helmet
to the aid of his lord, uttered few words:
'Beloved Beowulf, bear all things well!
You gave it out long ago in your youth
that, living, you would not allow your glory
ever to abate. Bold-tempered chieftain,
famed for your deeds, you must defend your life now
with all your strength. I shall help you.'

When these words had been spoken, the worm came on
    wrathful,
attacked a second time, terrible visitant,
sought out his foes in a surge of flame,
the hated men.
                    Mail-shirt did not serve
the young spear-man; and shield was withered
back to the boss by the billow of fire;
but when the blazing had burnt up his own,
the youngster stepped smartly to take

the cover of his kinsman's. Then did that kingly warrior
remember his deeds again and dealt out a sword-blow
with his full strength: it struck into the head
with annihilating weight. But Nailing snapped,
failed in the battle, Beowulf's sword
of ancient grey steel. It was not granted to him
that an iron edge could ever lend him
help in a battle; his hand was too strong.
I have heard that any sword, however hardened by wounds,
that he bore into battle, his blow would overtax
– any weapon whatever; it was the worse for him.

A third time the terrible fire-drake
remembered the feud. The foe of the people
rushed in on the champion when a chance offered:
seething with warspite, he seized his whole neck
between bitter fangs: blood covered him,
Beowulf's life-blood, let in streams.
Then I heard how the earl alongside the king
in the hour of need made known the valour,
boldness and strength that were bred in him.
His hand burned as he helped his kinsman,
but the brave soldier in his splendid armour
ignored the head and hit the attacker
somewhat below it, so that the sword went in,
flashing-hilted; and the fire began
to slacken in consequence.
                    The king once more
took command of his wits, caught up a stabbing-knife
of the keenest battle-sharpness, that he carried in his harness:
and the Geats' Helm struck through the serpent's body.

So daring drove out life: they had downed their foe
by common action, the atheling pair,
and had made an end of him. So in the hour of need

a warrior must live. For the lord this was
the last victory in the list of his deeds
and works in the world. The wound that the earth-drake
had first succeeded in inflicting on him
began to burn and swell; he swiftly felt
the bane beginning to boil in his chest,
the poison within him. The prince walked across
to the side of the barrow, considering deeply;
he sat down on a ledge, looked at the giant-work,
saw how the age-old earth-hall contained
stone arches anchored on pillars.
Then that excellent thane with his own hands washed
his battle-bloodied prince, bathed with water
the famous leader, his friend and lord,
sated with fighting; he unfastened his helmet.

Beowulf spoke; he spoke through the pain
of his fatal wound. He well knew
that he had come to the end of his allotted days,
his earthly happiness; all the number
of his days had disappeared: death was very near.
'I would now wish to give my garments in battle
to my own son, if any such
after-inheritor, an heir of my body,
had been granted to me. I have guarded this people
for half a century; not a single ruler
of all the nations neighbouring about
has dared to affront me with his friends in war,
or threaten terrors. What the times had in store for me

I awaited in my homeland; I held my own,
sought no secret feud, swore very rarely
a wrongful oath. In all of these things,
sick with my life's wound, I may still rejoice:
for when my life shall leave my body

the Ruler of Men may not charge me
with the slaughter of kinsmen.

                              Quickly go now,
beloved Wiglaf, and look upon the hoard
under the grey stone, now the serpent lies dead,
sleeps rawly wounded, bereft of his treasure.
Make haste, that I may gaze upon that golden inheritance,
that ancient wealth; that my eyes may behold
the clear skilful jewels: more calmly then may I
on the treasure's account take my departure
of life and of the lordship I have long held.'

Straightaway, as I have heard, the son of Weoxstan
obeyed his wounded lord, weak from the struggle.
Following these words, he went in his ring-coat,
his broidered battle-tunic, under the barrow's roof.
Traversing the ledge to the treasure-house of jewels
the brave young thane was thrilled by the sight
of the gold gleaming on the ground where it lay,
the devices by the wall and the den of the serpent,
winger of the darkness. Drinking-cups stood there,
the unburnished vessels of a vanished race,
their ornaments awry. Old and tarnished
were the rows of helmets and the heaps of arm-rings,
twisted with cunning. Treasure can easily,
gold in the ground, get the better of
one of human race, hide it who will!
High above the hoard there hung, as he also saw,
a standard all woven wonderfully in gold,
the finest of finger-linkages: the effulgence it gave
allowed him to see the surface of the ground
and examine the treasures. No trace of the worm
was to be seen there, for the sword had finished him.

I heard of the plundering of the hoard in the knoll,
that ancient Giant-work, by that one man;
he filled his bosom with such flagons and vessels
as he himself chose; he took the standard also,
best of banners.

             Old Beowulf's sword,
iron of edge, had already struck
the creature who had been keeper of the treasures
for so long an age, employing his fire-blast
in the hoard's defence, flinging out its heat
in the depth of the nights; he died at last, violently.

The envoy made haste in his eagerness to return,
urged on by his prizes. He was pressed by anxiety
as to whether he would find his fearless man,
the lord of the Geats, alive in the open
where he had left him, lacking in strength.
Carrying the treasures, he came upon his prince,
the famous king, covered in blood
and at his life's end; again he began
to sprinkle him with water, until this word's point
broke through the breast-hoard.

                   The battle-king spoke,
an aged man in sorrow; he eyed the gold.
'I wish to put in words my thanks
to the King of Glory, the Giver of All,
the Lord of Eternity, for these treasures that I see,
that I should have been able to acquire for my people
before my death-day an endowment such as this.
My life's full portion I have paid out now
for this hoard of treasure; you must attend to the people's
needs henceforward; no further may I stay.
Bid men of battle build me a tomb
fair after fire, on the foreland by the sea

that shall stand as a reminder of me to my people,
towering high above Hronesness
so that ocean travellers shall afterwards name it
Beowulf's barrow, bending in the distance
their masted ships through the mists upon the sea.'

He unclasped the golden collar from his neck,
staunch-hearted prince, and passed it to the thane,
with the gold-plated helmet, harness and arm-ring;
he bade the young spear-man use them well:
'You are the last man left of our kindred,
the house of the Waymundings! Weird has lured
each of my family to his fated end,
each earl through his valour; I must follow them.'

This was the aged man's uttermost word
from the thoughts of his breast; he embraced the pyre's
seething surges; soul left its case,
going its way to the glory of the righteous.

How wretchedly it went with the warrior then,
the younger soldier, when he saw on the ground
his best-beloved at his life's end
suffering miserably! The slayer lay also
bereft of life, beaten down in ruin,
terrible earth-drake. He was unable any longer
to rule the ring-hoard, the writhing serpent,
since the hammer's legacy, hard and battle-scarred,
the iron edges, had utterly destroyed him;
the far-flier lay felled along the ground
beside his store-house, still from his wounds.
He did not mount the midnight air,
gliding and coiling, glorying in his hoard,
flaunting his aspect; he fell to the earth
at the powerful hand of that prince in war.

Not one of the men of might in that land,
however daring in deeds of every kind,
had ever succeeded, from all I have heard,
in braving the venomous breath of that foe
or putting rude hands on the rings in that hall
if his fortune was to find the defender of the barrow
waiting and on his guard. The gaining of the hoard
of beautiful treasure was Beowulf's death;
so it was that each of them attained the end
of his life's lease.

          It was not long then
till they budged from the wood, the battle-shirkers,
ten of them together, those traitors and weaklings
who had not dared deploy their spears
in their own lord's extreme need.
They bore their shields ashamedly,
their armour of war, to where the old man lay.
They regarded Wiglaf. Wearily he sat,
a foot-soldier, at the shoulder of his lord,
trying to wake him with water; but without success.
For all his desiring it, he was unable to hold
his battle-leader's life in this world
or affect anything of the All-Wielder's;
for every man's action was under the sway
of God's judgement, just as it is now.

There was a rough and a ready answer
on the young man's lips for those who had lost their nerve;
Wiglaf spoke, Weoxstan's offspring,
looked at them unlovingly, and with little joy at heart:
'A man who would speak the truth may say with justice
that a lord of men who allowed you those treasures,
who bestowed on you the trappings that you stand there in
– as, at the ale-bench, he would often give

to those who sat in hall both helmet and mail-shirt
as a lord to his thanes, and things of the most worth
that he was able to find anywhere in the world
– that he had quite thrown away and wasted cruelly
all that battle-harness when the battle came upon him.
The king of our people had no cause to boast
of his companions of the guard. Yet God vouchsafed him,
the Master of Victories, that he should avenge himself
when courage was wanted, by his weapon single-handed.
I was little equipped to act as body-guard
for him in the battle, but, above my own strength,
I began all the same to support my kinsman.
Our deadly enemy grew ever the weaker –
when I had struck him with my sword – less strongly welled
the fire from his head. Too few supporters
flocked to our prince when affliction came.
Now there shall cease for your race the receiving of
    treasure,
the bestowal of swords, all satisfaction of ownership,
all comfort of home. Your kinsmen every one,
shall become wanderers without land-rights
as soon as athelings over the world
shall hear the report of how you fled,
a deed of ill fame. Death is better
for any earl than an existence of disgrace!'

He bade that the combat's result be proclaimed in the city
over the brow of the headland; there the band of earls
had sat all morning beside their shields
in heavy spirits, half expecting
that it would be the last day of their beloved man,
half hoping for his return. The rider from the headland
in no way held back the news he had to tell;

as his commission was, he called out over all:
'The Lord of the Geats lies now on his slaughter-bed,
the leader of the Weathers, our loving provider,
dwells in his death-rest through the dragon's power.
Stretched out beside him, stricken with the knife,
lies his deadly adversary. With the edge of the sword
he could not contrive, try as he might,
to wound the monster. Weoxtan's son
Wiglaf abides with Beowulf there,
one earl waits on the other one lifeless;
in weariness of heart he watches by the heads
of friend and foe.
                    The fall of the king,
when it spreads abroad and is spoken of
among the Frisians and the Franks, forebodes a time
of wars for our people. The war against the Hugas
had a hard beginning when Hygelac sailed
into the land of the Frisians with his fleet-army:
there it was that the Hetware hurled themselves upon him
and with their greater strength stoutly compelled
that battle-clad warrior to bow before them;
he fell among the troop, distributed no arms
as lord to the guard. It has not been granted to us since
to receive mercy from the Merovingian king.

Nor can I expect peace or fair dealing
from the Swedish nation; it is no secret
that it was Ongentheow who put an end to the life
of Hrethel's son, Hathkin, by Hrefnawudu
when in their pride the people of the Geats
first made attack upon the fighting Scylfings.
Quickly did the formidable father of Ohthere,
terrible veteran, return that blow,
he cut down the sea-king, recaptured his wife,

the mother of Onela and Ohthere in her youth,
now an aged woman, her ornaments stripped from her.
He then drove after his deadly foes
so that they hid themselves, hard-pressed,
in the Ravenswood, and without a lord.

    With his host he besieged those whom swords had left
ailing from their wounds. All through the night
he promised horrors to that unhappy band,
saying that on the morrow he would mutilate them
with the edges of the sword, and string some up on the
   gallows
as sport for the birds. With break of day
what comfort came to those care-oppressed men
when they heard Hygelac's horn and trumpet
giving voice, as that valiant man came up
with the flower of his host, following on their tracks!

    The bloody swathe of the Swedes and the Geats
in their slaughterous pursuit could be seen from afar
– how the peoples had stirred up the strife between them.
The earl Ongentheow took the upper ground;
the wise champion went up to his stronghold
in the van of his kinsmen; the veteran grieved,
but he knew the power of the superb Hygelac,
his strength in war; he was not confident
of his resistance, that he could stand against the vikings,
defend his hoard against the fighters from the sea,
his children and his queen. He chose to draw back,
old behind his earth-wall.
                Then was the offering of the chase
to the people of the Swedes; sweeping forward,
the standards of Hygelac surged over the camp
as Hrethel's brood broke through the rampart.
Then was Ongentheow the ashen-haired

brought to bay by the brightness of swords
and the king of a nation must kneel as Eofor
singly disposed. It was a desperate blow
that Wulf Wonreding's weapon fetched him,
and at the stroke streams of blood
sprang forth beneath his hair. The hoary-headed Scylfing,
undismayed by this deadly blow,
gave in exchange a graver stroke
as he came round to face him, king of the people.
Wonred's brave son was incapable
of the answer-blow upon the older man,
for the king had cut through the casque on his head,
forced him to bend; he bowed to the earth
marked with blood. Yet he was not marked for death;
it was a keen wound, but he recovered from it.
Then as his brother lay there, the brave Eofor,
Hygelac's follower, fetched his broad sword,
an ancient giant-blade, to the giant-helm of Ongentheow
above his shield, and split it; then the shepherd of the people,
the king, fell down, fatally wounded.

There were many to bind up the brother's wounds;
they raised him at once, now the way was open
and the battlefield had fallen to them.
One sturdy warrior then stripped the other,
took from Ongentheow his iron war-shirt,
his hilted sword and his helmet also,
the old man's accoutrement, and carried it to Hygelac.
He accepted the harness with a handsome promise
of rewards among the people; a promise he kept.
For at his homecoming Hrethel's offspring
rewarded Eofor and Wulf for their assault
with copious treasures. The king of the Geats
handed to each of them a hundred thousand

in lands and linked rings; there was little cause for any
on middle earth to begrudge them these glories earned in
  battle.
He also gave to Eofor his only daughter,
a grace to his home and a guarantee of favour.

      It is this feud, this fierce hostility,
this murder-lust between men, I am moved to think,
that the Swedish people will prosecute against us
when once they learn that life has fled
from the lord of the Geats, guardian for so long
of hoard and kingdom, of keen shield-warriors
against every foe. Since the fall of the princes
he has taken care of our welfare, and accomplished yet more
heroic deeds.
                    Haste is best now,
that we should go to look on the lord of the people,
then bring our ring-bestower on his road,
escort him to the pyre. More than one portion of wealth
shall melt with the hero, for there's a hoard of treasure
and gold uncounted; a grim purchase,
for in the end it was with his own life
that he bought these rings: which the burning shall devour,
the fire enfold. No fellow shall wear
an arm-ring in his memory; no maiden's neck
shall be enhanced in beauty by the bearing of these rings.
Bereft of gold, rather, and in wretchedness of mind
she shall tread continually the tracks of exile
now that the leader of armies has laid aside his mirth,
his sport and glad laughter. Many spears shall therefore
feel cold in the mornings to the clasping fingers
and the hands that raise them. Nor shall the harper's melody
arouse them for battle; and yet the black raven,
quick on the marked men, shall have much to speak of

when he tells the eagle of his takings at the feast
where he and the wolf bared the bodies of the slain.'

Such was the rehearsal of the hateful tidings
by that bold messenger; amiss in neither
words nor facts. The war-band arose;
they went unhappily under Earna-ness
to look on the wonder with welling tears.
They found him on the sand, his soul fled,
keeping his resting-place: rings he had given them
in former times! But the final day
had come for the champion; and the chief of the Geats,
the warrior-king, had met his wondrous death.

Stranger the creature they encountered first
in the level place – the loathsome worm
stretched out opposite. Scorched by its own flames
lay the fire-drake in its fatal markings,
and it measured fifty feet as it lay.
He had once been master of the midnight air,
held sweet sway there, and swooped down again
to seek his den; now death held him fast,
he had made his last use of lairs in the earth.

Standing by him there were bowls and flagons,
there were platters lying there, and precious swords,
quite rusted through, as they had rested there
a thousand winters in the womb of earth.

And this gold of former men was full of power,
the huge inheritance, hedged about with a spell:
no one among men was permitted to touch
that golden store of rings unless God Himself,
the true King of Victories, the Protector of mankind,
enabled one He chose to open the hoard,
whichever among men should seem meet to Him.

It was plain to see then that this plan had failed
the creature who had kept these curious things hidden
wrongfully within the wall; the warden had slain
a man like few others; but the feud was straightaway
avenged and wrathfully. It is a wonder to know
where the most courageous of men may come to the end
of his alloted life, and no longer dwell
a man in the mead-hall among companions!

So it was for Beowulf when he embarked on that quarrel,
sought out the barrow-guard; he himself did not know
in what way his parting from the world was to come.
The great princes who had placed the treasure there
had laid on it a curse to last until doomsday,
that the man who should plunder the place would thereby
commit a crime, and be confined with devils,
tortured grievously in the trammels of hell.
But Beowulf had not looked on the legacy of these men
with too eager an eye, for all its gold.

Wiglaf spoke, Weoxstan's son:
'Many must often endure distress
for the sake of one; so it is now with us.
We could not urge any reason
on our beloved king, the keeper of the land,
why he should not approach the protector of the gold
but let him lie where he had long been already
and abide in his den until the end of the world.
He held to his high destiny.

                The hoard has been seen
that was acquired at such a cost; too cruel the fate
that impelled the king of the people towards it!
I myself was inside there, and saw all
the wealth of the chamber once my way was open
– little courtesy was shown in allowing me to pass

beneath the earth-wall. I urgently filled
my hands with a huge heap of the treasures
stored in the cave, carried them out
to my lord here. He was alive still
and commanded his wits. Much did he say
in his grief, the old man; he asked me to speak to you,
ordered that on the place of the pyre you should raise
a barrow fitting your friend's achievements;
conspicuous, magnificent, as among men he was
while he could wield the wealth of his stronghold
the most honoured of warriors on the wide earth.

Let us now hasten to behold again,
and approach once more that mass of treasures,
awesome under the walls; I shall guide you
so that from near at hand you may behold sufficiently
the thick gold and the bracelets. Let a bier be made ready,
contrive it quickly, so that when we come out again
we may take up our king, carry the man
beloved by us to his long abode
where he must rest in the Ruler's keeping.'

Then the son of Weoxstan, worthy in battle,
had orders given to owners of homesteads
and a great many warriors, that the governors of the people
from far and wide should fetch in wood
for the hero's funeral pyre.
                         'Now the flames shall grow dark
and the fire destroy the sustainer of the warriors
who often endured the iron shower
when, string-driven, the storm of arrows
sang over shield-wall, and the shaft did its work
urged on by its feathers, furthered the arrow-head.'

Then in his wisdom Weoxstan's son
called out from the company of the king's own thanes
seven men in all, who excelled among them,
and, himself the eighth warrior, entered in beneath
that unfriendly roof. The front-stepping man
bore in his hand a blazing torch.

When the men perceived a piece of the hoard
that remained unguarded, mouldering there
on the floor of the chamber, they did not choose by lot
who should remove it; undemurring,
as quickly as they could, they carried outside
the precious treasures; and they pushed the dragon,
the worm, over the cliff, let the waves take him
and the flood engulf the guardian of the treasures.
The untold profusion of twisted gold
was loaded onto a wagon, and the warrior prince
borne hoary-headed to Hronesness.

The Geat race then reared up for him
a funeral pyre. It was not a petty mound,
but shining mail-coats and shields of war
and helmets hung upon it, as he had desired.
Then the heroes, lamenting, laid out in the middle
their great chief, their cherished lord.
On top of the mound the men then kindled
the biggest of funeral-fires. Black wood-smoke
arose from the blaze, and the roaring of flames
mingled with weeping. The winds lay still
as the heat at the fire's heart consumed
the house of bone. And in heavy mood
they uttered their sorrow at the slaughter of their lord.

A woman of the Geats in grief sang out
the lament for his death. Loudly she sang,

her hair bound up, the burden of her fear
that evil days were destined her
– troops cut down, terror of armies,
bondage, humiliation. Heaven swallowed the smoke.

Then the Storm-Geat nation constructed for him
a stronghold on the headland, so high and broad
that seafarers might see it from afar.
The beacon to that battle-reckless man
they made in ten days. What remained from the fire
they cast a wall around, of workmanship
as fine as their wisest men could frame for it.
They placed in the tomb both the torques and the jewels,
all the magnificence that the men had earlier
taken from the hoard in hostile mood.
They left the earls' wealth in the earth's keeping,
the gold in the dirt. It dwells there yet,
of no more use to men than in ages before.

Then the warriors rode around the barrow,
twelve of them in all, athelings' sons.
They recited a dirge to declare their grief,
spoke of the man, mourned their King.
They praised his manhood and the prowess of his hands,
they raised his name; it is right a man
should be lavish in honouring his lord and friend,
should love him in his heart when the leading-forth
from the house of flesh befalls him at last.

This was the manner of the mourning of the men of the
    Geats,
sharers in the feast, at the fall of their lord:
they said that he was of all the world's kings
the gentlest of men, and the most gracious,
the kindest to his people, the keenest for fame.

THE FIGHT AT FINNSBURGH

THE only text of this fragment appears in George Hickes's *Linguarum Veterum Septentrionalium Thesaurus Grammatico-Criticus et Archaeologicus* (Oxoniae, 1705). Hickes found it on a leaf bound up with a collection of homilies in Lambeth Palace library; this leaf has unfortunately been lost.

The fragment is the story of a night attack made on a hall, and of the five days' defence made by Hnæf and his men. But why the attack was made, or by whom, would not have been known without the evidence of the Finn lay in *Beowulf* (ll. 1068ff.)

The fragment begins in the middle of a speech by a man guarding the door of Hnæf's hall.

'. . . the horns of the house, hall-gables burning?'

Battle-young Hnæf broke silence:
'It is not the eaves aflame, nor in the east yet
does day break; no dragon flies this way.
It is the soft clashing of claymores you hear
that they carry to the house.

                Soon shall be the cough of birds,
hoar wolf's howl, hard wood-talk,
shield's answer to shaft.

                  Now shines the moon,
welkin-wanderer. The woes at hand
shall bring to the full this folk's hatred for us.

    Awake! on your feet! Who fights for me?
Hold your lindens right, hitch up your courage,
think bravely, be with me at the doors!'

The Fight at Finnsburgh

The gold-clad thanes rose, girt on their swords.
Two doubtless soldiers stepped to the door,
Sigeferth and Eaha, with their swords out,
and Ordlaf and Guthlaf to the other door went,
Hengest himself hastening in their steps.

Hearing these adversaries advance on the door
Guthere held on to Garulf so he should not
front the rush to force the threshold
and risk his life, whose loss could not be remedied;
but clear above their whispers he called out his demand,
– brave heart – 'Who held the door?'

'My name is Sigeferth, of the Secgan, chief,
known through the seas. I have seen a few fights
and can take on trouble. What you intend for me
your own flesh shall be the first to taste.'

Then swung strokes sounded along the wall;
wielded by the brave, the bone-shielding
boss-boards split. Burg-floor spoke,
and Garulf fell at last in the fighting at the door,
Garulf, the first man in the Frisian islands,
son to Guthlaf, and good men lay around,
a pale crowd of corpses. The crows dangled
black and brown. Blades clashing
flashed fire – as though all Finnsburgh were ablaze.

Never have sixty swordmen in a set fight
borne themselves more bravely; or better I have not heard
    of.
Never was the bright mead better earned
than that which Hnæf gave his guard of youth.

They fought and none fell. On the fifth day
the band was still whole and still held the doors.

Then a wounded warrior went to the side,
said his ring-coat was riven to pieces,
stout hauberk though it was, and that his helm had gone
    through.

The folk's shepherd and shielder asked him
how the braves bore their wounds
and which of the young men . . .

BIBLIOGRAPHY

Klaeber includes a fifty-eight-page bibliography of *Beowulf* studies up to 1936, and Chambers is also useful. Recent work is reviewed in *The Year's Work in English Studies* (Oxford, published annually for the English Association). Works cited elsewhere in this volume under the author's name are included here, but the following list is otherwise selective and personal.

Facsimile

DAVIS, N. *Beowulf*, a facsimile with facing transcription. The Early English Text Society, Oxford, 1966.

Editions

KLAEBER, F. *Beowulf and the Fight at Finnsburg*, edited with Introduction, Bibliography, Notes, Glossary, and Appendices, 3rd edn with two supplements, Boston and London, 1951.

WRENN, C. L. *Beowulf with the Finnesburg Fragment*, 2nd edn, London, 1958.

Translations

GARMONSWAY, G. N., and SIMPSON, J. *Beowulf and its Analogues*, London and New York, 1968.

CLARK HALL, J., and WRENN, C. L. *Beowulf and the Finnesburg Fragment*, a Translation into Modern English Prose, with Prefatory Remarks by J. R. R. Tolkien. 2nd edn, London, 1950.

Studies

BLISS, A. J. *The Metre of Beowulf*, Oxford, 1968.

BONJOUR, A. *The Digressions in Beowulf*, Oxford, 1950.

CHAMBERS, R. W. *Beowulf, an Introduction*, with a supplement by C. L. Wrenn, 3rd edn, Cambridge, England, 1963. See also his '*Beowulf* and the Heroic Age in England' in *Man's Unconquerable Mind*, London, 1939.

SISAM, K. *The Structure of Beowulf*, Oxford, 1965.

TOLKIEN, J. R. R. *Beowulf: the Monsters and the Critics*, Oxford, 1937.
WHITELOCK, D. *The Audience of Beowulf*, Oxford, 1951.

The Epic

ARISTOTLE. *Poetics* in *Literary Criticism: Plato to Dryden*, ed. A. H. Gilbert, Detroit, 1962.
BOWRA, C. M. *Heroic Poetry*, London, 1952.
   Primitive Song, London, 1962.
CHADWICK, H. M., and N. K. *The Growth of Literature*, 3 vols., Cambridge, England, 1932.
FRYE, N. *Anatomy of Criticism*, Princeton, 1957.
KER, W. P. *Epic and Romance*, London, 1908.
   The Dark Ages, London, 1904.
KIRK, G. S. *Homer and the Epic*, Cambridge, England, 1965.
LORD, A. B. *The Singer of Tales*, Harvard, 1964. See also his 'Beowulf and the Odyssey' in *Mediæval and Linguistic Studies in honour of F. P. Magoun, Jr*, ed. J. Bessinger and R. Creed, Cambridge, Mass., 1968.
NOTOPOULOS, J. A. 'Studies in Early Greek Poetry', *Harvard Studies in Classical Philology*, lxii, Cambridge, Mass., 1964.
PARRY, M. *The Making of Homeric Verse*, ed. A. Parry, Oxford, 1971.

Anglo-Saxon Art

BLAIR, P. HUNTER. *Introduction to Anglo-Saxon England*, Cambridge, England, 1956.
BRUCE-MITFORD, R. L. S. *The Sutton Hoo Ship Burial*, London, 1968.
WILSON, D. M. *The Anglo-Saxons*, revised edn, London, 1971.

Other works cited

BEDE. *A History of the English Church and People*, translated by Leo Sherley-Price, revised by R. E. Latham, Harmondsworth, 1968.
GRETTISSAGA. *The Saga of Grettir the Strong*, translated by G. A. Hight, ed. P. Foote, London, 1968.
HESIOD. *The Works and Days*, translated by Dorothea Wender, Harmondsworth, 1972.
HOMER. *The Iliad*, translated by R. Lattimore, Ann Arbor, 1960.
   The Odyssey, translated by R. Fitzgerald, London, 1965.
SEBEOK, T. (ed.). *Myth: A Symposium*, Bloomington, 1968.

NOTES

THE translation is based upon the text and apparatus of Klaeber, though I have followed a few of Wrenn's suggestions. I rely on their texts completely, and my construction of the text also leans heavily on them. I have consulted the manuscript and Davis's facsimile; but the student of *Beowulf* owes his entire primary understanding of the text to the editors, scholars and philologists.

The notes offered here aim at clearing up the more obvious difficulties in understanding the progress of the poem as here translated. Though all line references are to the text of Klaeber, the glosses provided refer primarily to this translation and not to the original. There is no room here to explain readings of the text or simplifications of some near-synonymous alternative forms of proper names; nor do I give alternative interpretations of controverted passages. Students of the original will, I trust, be able to see what I have done.

These notes should be used in conjunction with the Introduction and the Index of Proper Names (p. 173).

Introduction
1. Sisam, p. 1.
2. Hesiod, *The Works and Days*, 156–66, Dorothea Wender's translation.
3. See Chambers, pp. 41 ff. For a general account of the battle between solar mythologists and sceptics, see R. M. Dorson in Sebeok, p. 25.
4. Frye, p. 139.
5. Aristotle, *Poetics*, cap. XXIV, p. 105.
6. See Tolkien on the poem's relation to the world-view of Norse mythology.
7. Sebeok, pp. 89–90. Levi-Strauss's analysis of the Oedipus myth suggested this lay-out to me.
8. For *The Dream of the Rood* see Alexander, p. 103.

9. Translated in J. P. Clancy's *The Earliest Welsh Poetry*, London, 1970.

10. Bede, pp. 250–53.

11. See especially Kirk and Notopoulos.

12. Bliss, p. 109.

1. The epic 'oral' beginning promises a recital of the deeds of the Danish royal house. The miraculous arrival of Scyld, eponymous founder of the Scylding dynasty, brings joy, his departure sorrow, to the Danes. The infant found on the shore (like Moses in the bulrushes) becomes the 'shield' of his people and brings them prosperity (the significance of Sheaf?) and security in the form of a son and heir, Beow. Beow ('Beowulf the Dane', 53) is not to be confused with Beowulf the Geat, hero of the poem, introduced at 343.

That the account of the funeral is accurate enough is shown by the richness and composition of the treasure-hoard in the buried funeral ship found in 1939 at Sutton Hoo, the royal burying ground of the East Anglian dynasty of the Wuffings. The Sutton Hoo ship contains no body; it is thought to be a pagan memorial to the Christian king, Anna (d. 656). The hoard is now in the British Museum. See Garmondsway, Smyser, Bruce-Mitford.

43. 'Not less great' – i.e. vastly greater, since the child was 'unaccommodated'. A characteristic understatement.

82a–83b. Literally, 'it awaited the destructive surges of hostile fire.' A dark allusion to the eventual burning-down of Heorot by the Heathobards. Hrothgar is to marry his daughter Freawaru to Ingeld the Heathobard. But, as Beowulf foretells at 2022 ff., the Heathobards will not forget that Ingeld's father, Froda, had been killed by the Danes. That stories of Ingeld were well-known (and that the audience might be expected to take the point of this allusion) is suggested by the letter of Bishop Alcuin to the monks of Lindisfarne in 797, in which he asks '*Quid Hinieldus cum Christo?*' 'What has Ingeld got to do with Christ?' (The monks had been listening to heathen stories in the refectory.)

86–114. The Creation, Cain and Abel and the Giants are of course taken from Genesis. For the comparable story of Caedmon see Bede, 206–7.

142. Grendel is called the 'new hall-thane' with shuddering irony: the poet jealously records thus any usurpation of the rights of ownership or of hospitality. Nor should it have been so 'easy' to find hearth-companions 'among the outer buildings' (138).

156. The civilized way of settling a feud was by a compensatory payment of *wergild*, a man's worth in money. Grendel is not interested.

194. Beowulf is introduced as Hygelac's thane: the function precedes the name, as with Heorot, Grendel, Wulfgar.

460. Nothing is known of the circumstances in which Beowulf's father set off the feud between the Geats and the Wylfings. The young Hrothgar paid the *wergild* for Heatholaf, something evidently beyond the means of Edgetheow or his people. Beowulf repays Hrothgar by ending the Grendel-feud.

499. Unferth. The name means 'Un-peace': the drunken Unferth provokes strife by doubting the veracity of his master's guest. This sets up Beowulf with a grand opportunity to disclose himself as a slayer of underwater monsters, which paves the way for the later Mere-Fight and the feat of swimming by which Beowulf escapes from Friesland. Unferth plays a role similar to that of Laodamas in the *Odyssey* (viii, 158ff.). (For a comparison of *Beowulf* and the *Odyssey* see Lord in *Magoun Studies*.) Unferth is also 'anti-peace' in that he has killed his own kindred (587ff.; cf. Cain, Hathkin, Heremod, Hrothulf, Onela). He later offers Beowulf his sword, Hrunting, for the Mere-Fight; Hrunting's failure again sets up Beowulf with a chance to display further his strength and magnanimity.

515. 'The Spearman' – the sea. Neptune's trident?

569. The mention of the dawn or the sun often betokens glory for Beowulf (see 1570 and the note on 1880).

612. Wealhtheow, Hrothgar's queen, is the very pattern of a hostess, and her daughter takes after her. She moves through the hall among the young men and the older men, offering the cup (cf. *Gnomic Verses*, Alexander, p. 87). In the patriarchal warrior aristocracy of the poem, women, valued for all the peaceful virtues, feature incidentally as beautiful, as companions of the bed, as widows or as shrews; but primarily they are hostesses or 'peace-weavers' – daughters used to heal a breach by a marriage-alliance, as with

Hildeburgh and Freawaru. Accepting the hospitable cup, Beowulf makes on it the third of his four Grendel-vows.

668. Beowulf is now 'monster-guard': the epithet of function confers identity. The apposition in 670 is characteristic, and revealing.

681. Grendel's inability to use a sword is uncivilized; like his lack of table-manners, it is a mark of his incomplete humanity. Part man, part monster, Grendel's exact appearance is wisely left indefinite. He is fittingly huge and weapon-proof, has a hand with talons like steel, a magic glove and hellish eyes – he is a monster and a fiend. But he is also human. Glam in *Grettissaga*, with his elbows on the cross-beam looking down at Grettir in bed, is a more definite figure.

741. Why does Beowulf allow Grendel to devour his companion Handscio? Perhaps it was felt necessary to involve Beowulf in the feud personally; perhaps Handscio is a sacrificial figure, like Protesilaos or Palinurus or Elpenor – or the viking who first steps onto the causeway at Maldon (Alexander, p. 116).

780. The apparent indestructibility of the hall is partly magical. Intricate art is always accorded 'wonder' in *Beowulf*: see the building of the dragon's barrow and of Beowulf's barrow; the manufacture of weapons, armour, cups and adornments; and the skill of the *scop* – the artificer-poet (e.g. 89ff., 870ff.). Well-made things can be handed down, and the undoing of Heorot would be the undoing of Danish society.

814b–815a. Many of the clinching points of *Beowulf* are made in these epigrammatic juxtapositions; they are usually untranslatable.

825. The notion of 'cleansing' is also expressed at 432, 1176, 1620 and 2352.

829. The performance of a vow is always a justifiable occasion for pride.

875. The lay of Beowulf's new exploit is followed by a recital of Sigemund's deeds, told very summarily: 'he was by far the most famous of adventurers', 898. The point of the allusion is taken to be the difference between the dragon-fights of Sigemund and Beowulf: Sigemund kills his dragon alone 'under the grey rock', and takes the gold away in his boat. The listeners would know that there was a curse upon this gold, from which Sigemund eventually died; they would also know that Beowulf will die in his dragon-fight and will

not sail away with the gold. So the compliment conceals a tragic irony. (Sigemund is better known to us as William Morris's *Sigurd the Volsung*, a rumbustious rendering of the *Volsungasaga*; the dragon-fight is attributed to Siegfried in the *Nibelungenlied* and in Wagner.)

901–15. Heremod is here introduced – rather schematically – as a foil to Beowulf. He appears as a tyrannical Danish king (presumably Scyld's predecessor) who notoriously went to the bad after a glorious youth – the exact opposite to Beowulf. In 1709–22 Hrothgar holds him up to Beowulf as a dreadful warning.

980ff. The sight of Grendel's whole grip reduces Unferth to an unwonted silence.

1017. Hrothulf, the son of Hrothgar's brother Halga, apparently shares the throne. The poet harps on the ultimate dissolution of their friendship: Hrothulf is to usurp the succession after Hrothgar's death.

1025–6. An understatement: Beowulf gloried in his prizes.

1068–9. The lay of Finn. Part of the story summarized here is told in the fragmentary Anglo-Saxon poem, *The Fight at Finnsburg* (p. 153). The story in outline – reduced to order – is as follows: Hnæf, a Dane (or 'Half-Dane') is visiting his sister Hildeburgh, who is married to Finn, the king of the Frisians (also called Jutes). The Frisians treacherously attack the Danes in the night, and kill both Hnæf and Hildeburgh's son. The surviving Danes, led by Hengest, force Finn to accept a compromise whereby the Danes are to become followers of Finn on equal terms with the Frisians. To serve one's lord's slayer is of course flat against the Germanic code, and Hengest cannot 'decline the accustomed remedy' (1142) when the son of Hunlaf places a famous sword across his knees. He is bound to take vengence for Hnæf. Guthlaf and Oslaf, who have been to Denmark and re-turned again, taunt Finn with his treachery and provoke the final fight. Finn is slain, Hildeburgh taken home; vengeance has success-fully been taken by the Danes. At a cost.

The moral would seem to be Beowulf's remark at 2029 that 'When a lord is dead/It is seldom that the slaying-spear sleeps for long,/ Seldom indeed – dear though the bride may be.' Hildeburgh and Freawaru are Danish brides who fail to mend ancient feuds.

1159–68. The revelry and rejoicing continue; but the tableau of the patriarch Hrothgar supported by Hrothulf and Unferth inspires little confidence after a tale such as we have just heard. The doubts cast on Hrothulf's future and Unferth's past are borne out in Wealhtheow's speech. Lines 1163–8 are six-stress lines.

1169–91. Wealhtheow raises the question whether Hrothulf *will* remember Hrothgar's kindness when he is gone. The audience can be expected to think how Beowulf repays the kindness that Hrothgar (and Hrethel) showed him when he was a child. The tableau of Beowulf between the young Scyldings looks very much like a deliberate contrast to the earlier trio.

1195–1214. The collar is second only to the Brisings' necklace. Hama would seem to have stolen the necklace that the Brising firedwarves made for the goddess Freya from the Gothic tyrant Eormenric (see Klaeber). Any further point in this allusion has been lost. But the import of the fact that Hygelac was to wear the collar on his last expedition is clear enough. (Beowulf is represented as giving the collar to Hygd at 2172ff.: but this inconsistency, common in orally composed works, does not affect the macabre irony, deepened by the applause which now ensues.)

1215ff. If the interpretations offered above are correct, Wealhtheow's diplomatic speech requesting Beowulf to protect her sons must be full of a ghastly irony, of which she is presumably unconscious. The harmony of Heorot in which she rejoices is about to be shattered by the impending doom of Ashhere; and the eventual fate of her sons.

1240. *Beorscealca sum* could not apply to Beowulf, though the poet neglects to tell us that he did not sleep in Heorot.

1250b. Not an ironic line.

1258. The introduction of Grendel's Mother starts another cycle of destruction and defence, another stage in the feud: the descent from Cain and the Grendel fight are rehearsed again (and again by Hrothgar) because – in essence – the same thing is happening in the same fatal pattern. Cf. *Grettissaga*, Chapters 64–6.

1281. 'A sudden change' – *edhwyrft* – is the characteristic movement by which the wrestling-match between good and evil progresses. Cf. *gewrixl*, 1304 and *wyrp*, 1315.

1303–6. Reciprocity is maintained: Grendel kills Handscio, Beowulf kills Grendel and keeps his hand; Grendel's mother kills Ashhere

and takes the hand, Beowulf kills Grendel's mother. He brings back
Grendel's head as war-spoil in exchange for Ashhere's head.

1322. Ashhere is the ideal counsellor. *Beowulf* tends to put tradi-
tional generic character-types to edifying use: the conceptual ideal
becomes the moral ideal. The coastguard remains a coastguard; but
Wulfgar, Ashhere and Wiglaf are held up as models. Cf. Spenser's
letter to Ralegh in dedication of the *Faerie Queene*.

1357–76. Literary descriptions of hell are thought to have influenced
this landscape. Cf. *Grettissaga*, Chapter 88. The inconsistencies in the
description of the Mere have bothered sternly topographical critics.

1384–5. Not a Christian sentiment.

1420. The unnatural horror of the unburied head, the blood in the
water and the repulsive sea-monsters is banished magically by the
'bright phrases' of the horn (cf. the effects of Hygelac's horn at 3000).
The Gothic grisliness of their 'guest' is likewise quelled by the splen-
dour of the hero's arming. Unferth is once more a foil.

1516. The underwater hall has no hearth but an unnatural fire. The
progress of the fight is symmetrical: after Beowulf's sword fails, he
throws her to the ground; she then throws him, but her knife fails.
Beowulf, like Grendel, is immune to swords and ordinary swords are
useless to him.

1586. Grendel is dead. The metaphor of sleep is common in the
poem. Cf. also *The Dream of the Rood* (Alexander, p. 103). The his-
torical Danes cut off the head of the English King Edmund and of
Ealdorman Bryhtnoth.

1604. Compare the construction and the situation with 2895–6,
where the experienced warriors are right. Cf. also 1873–6.

1650. Cf. 1421, 1440. Also *Macbeth*, Act III, Scene 4.

1687. These are the Giants of 113–14 and of Genesis. For whom the
sword was made (1696) were a question worthy the conjecture of Sir
Thomas Browne.

1700–1784. Hrothgar's speech of congratulation to Beowulf con-
tains a substantial warning against the self-satisfied enjoyment of
worldly prosperity, illustrated by the career of Heremod and the
events of his own reign. Heremod's meanness and cruelty are typified
by the drunken murder of table-companions. Hrothgar himself is
not guilty of pride or closefistedness; his prosperity passes and in age

he endures 'grief after joy' (1775). The same thing is to happen to Beowulf. The moral psychology of the homily is Christian.

1880. In this poem of strong contrasts there is none more characteristic than that between the presageful grief of the aged Hrothgar at their parting and Beowulf's youthful joy in setting out for home.

In his moments of glory Beowulf is usually seen striding along in the sunlight, but never more unconsciously and vigorously than here. The journeys and voyages are the most Homeric passages in the poem, both in their unclouded briskness and in their palindromic pattern of construction. The procedures of launching and landing are bound to mirror each other in reverse, of course, like sunrise and sunset. But in the deployment of the coastguards, of the marching armoured men, and of the sighting of land, the poet is surely putting oral traditions of composition to conscious use.

1925. After Hrothgar and Wealhtheow, Hygelac and Hygd seem somewhat pinched; Geatland is weaker than Denmark and shows us the heroic life from the losing side.

1931b–1962. Offa and his queen. This Offa is the king of the Angles in their continental homeland, legendary ancestor of the historical Offa who was a famous king of Mercia in the eighth century. The compliments here paid Offa I have suggested that *Beowulf* passed through the court of Offa II.

2022. Chief of the new pieces of information in Beowulf's recital is his presentation of Freawaru rather than Wealhtheow as the hostess of Heorot. The point of introducing her is to allow Beowulf to voice his doubts about the marrying off of daughters to heal ancient feuds: Hrothgar does not seem to have drawn the right moral from the history of Hildeburgh's marriage to Finn. Heorot itself is eventually to be burnt down in vengeance for the killing of Froda, though Beowulf confines himself to imagining the beginning of this stage of the feud. The 'old spear-warrior' plays the part of prompter, like the son of Hunlaf at Finnsburgh. 'The other' (2061) is the son of Withergyld; after his act of revenge he conceals himself in the Heathobard lands. The wearer of Withergyld's sword does not awake from his sleep after the wedding-feast.

2085. Grendel's glove was not mentioned earlier; nor was Handscio's name given; but then, Beowulf's 'sluggish youth' and Hygelac's efforts to persuade him not to go to Denmark also come to us as a surprise. But we should not expect the consistency of a whodunnit in a protean tale full of wonders. Did Beowulf marry Hygd? We shall never know.

2158. Heorogar gave the armour to his brother rather than to his son.

2177–89. Beowulf heeds Hrothgar's advice: his career is the reverse of Heremod's. Nevertheless, time is to bring him another 'reversal' (2188).

2200. The last part of *Beowulf* begins *in medias res*, when the hero has succeeded Hygelac and Heardred and reigned fifty years. The *wrœcca* or adventurer is transformed into a patriarch and is confronted with his greatest adversary, the dragon. The dragon attacks the Geats because his hoard has been rifled by a slave; the slave had to rob the hoard so as to appease his lord's anger. The hoard is the treasure of an entire race, now extinct, who have laid a curse on anyone who should disturb it.

2155ff. This leaf of the MS. is damaged, and the text is incomplete and conjectural. The 'lay of the last survivor' (2247–66) is the most sustained example of the poem's habit of metonymy: the heroic way of life is seen in terms of its material prizes. Cf. *The Ruin, The Wanderer* (Alexander, pp. 29, 63).

2324. Though the poem embodies several attempts to 'explain' the dragon and the hoard, the explanation follows the given fact. Beowulf's immediate move to avenge the burning down of his hall is likewise a *donnée* of heroic story. He fears he may have angered God, but it is stressed that such dark thoughts were 'unaccustomed' (2332). Motivation is *post hoc*. The action is henceforward counter-pointed by ever greater and greater flashbacks.

2354b–2396. An expansion of the deaths mentioned in 2220–6. After Hygelac's death in Friesland (against the Hetware, Hugas and Merovingian Franks) Beowulf declines Hygd's offer of the kingdom. The ideal uncle, he serves Heardred as he had served his father. But in the Second Swedish War (recounted first) Heardred is killed by Onela, the wicked uncle of Eanmund and Eadgils, whom he has deprived of the Swedish throne; Heardred pays the penalty for offering them hospitality. Beowulf later helps Eadgils overthrow Onela.

2426–71. Hrethel married his only daughter to Edgetheow and brought up his grandson Beowulf like one of his own sons; Beowulf in return serves these sons loyally (unlike Hrothulf). The patriarch

Hrethel dies of grief after his eldest son Herebeald has accidentally been shot dead by the second son, Hathkin. Fratricide cannot be settled by *wergild* or by vengeance; Hrethel is compared with the powerless father of a hanged man. However, as Beowulf points out, he was at least able to leave the land of the Geats to his remaining sons.

2472-89. Hathkin's fratricidal arrow causes the tragic death of Hrethel, which in its turn is the signal for the Swedes to begin the First Swedish War. Ohthere and Onela, sons of the Swedish patriarch Ongentheow, ambush the Geats. A Geatish punitive expedition succeeds, but their king, Hathkin, is killed by Ongentheow; who in his turn is killed by Hathkin's brother, Hygelac, or rather by Hygelac's retainer, Eofor. This episode is treated fully at 2922-98.

2501. We may guess that it is with this sword, Nailing (2680), that Dayraven had killed Hygelac. Beowulf is essentially 'unarmed': the sword, like the shield, is useless to him; even armour only helps him underwater. True to his name, he crushes Dayraven to death.

2527. 'Grey rock' betokens death: see 887 (Sigemund and the fatal dragon's hoard), 1415 (Ashhere's head), 2744 (another fatal dragon's hoard).

2596ff. Comparison has been made between the companions and the apostles, and Wiglaf and Peter; but not, I think, between the slave and Judas. *Maldon* (77) is nearer: the companions flee to the wood (Alexander, p. 116). Wiglaf is, like Sigemund's Fitela, 'the young companion' – an ideal thane and kinsman, and a good listener. His father Weoxstan, fighting for the Swedish king Onela, killed Eanmund in the Second Swedish War. Weoxstan, a Scylfing and therefore a Swede, nevertheless leaves Eanmund's sword to Wiglaf 'among the Geats'. Weoxstan, Wiglaf and Beowulf all belong to the Waymundings, presumably a family of the Geat-Swedish border.

2729ff. Beowulf in his first dying speech rejoices in the thought of the protection he has given his people and in his blameless discharge of the duties of lordship; he has sworn a wrongful oath 'very rarely' (i.e. never); most crucial of all, he has slain no kinsmen. His desire to look on the gold he has won has sometimes been construed – or misconstrued – as blameworthy.

2764-6. This homiletic warning against avarice does not – strictly – seem to apply to Beowulf, Wiglaf, the Geats or even the slave. The taboo on grave-robbing, expressed in the curse on the gold, also seems of general rather than particular application. Heroic death is rewarded with heroic glory – gold – which the hero's people return to the ground in tribute to him.

2802ff. There is a remarkable resemblance between this and the account of the funeral pyre of Achilles and Patroclus described at *Odyssey* xxiv, 80ff.

2820. This unequivocally accords salvation to Beowulf.

2900. Like everything subsequent to the double death, the messenger's speech looks forward to imminent invasion by both the Swedes and the Franks and to the catastrophic defeat of the now lordless Geats (cf. the Danes after Heremod). After another allusion to Hygelac's fall in Friesland, we at last get a full picture of the First Swedish War. In the most vivid sequence in the poem, the logic of the feud is given clear expression in open narrative rather than allusion; in comparison with this, other episodes seem contrived for their exemplary value. After the 'bloody swathe' (2946) and the killing of the dragon-like Ongentheow (at the hands of two men) the messenger's conclusion at 2999 is irresistible.

3010ff. The dearly-bought gold is to be sacrificed with the body in tribute; the Geats will not profit by it, they will become the boast of the raven.

3051–7; 3069–75. A curse traditionally attaches to buried treasure. Whether it applies to Beowulf, the slave, the dragon, the Geats or the 'last survivor's' people who took the gold from the ground (2248) is not clear. Beowulf certainly dies, but the possibility that he is damned seems quite excluded by 2820 and 3074–5.

3077–84. That there were efforts to dissuade Beowulf (not previously mentioned, but cf. 1994ff.) is not meant to suggest that he was hubristic; simply to blame Bryhtnoth at Maldon or Roland at Roncesvalles is to misunderstand the point of heroic poetry.

3019. Compare Scyld's funeral at 27.

3126–9. The warriors were eager to take the gold, apparently out of enmity (3165a) rather than pleasure or fear.

3137ff. There are two stages: after a funeral similar to that of Hnæf the ashes, together with the (unburnt) gold, are placed in a barrow. See Klaeber's note and Smyser.

3166–8. That the gold in the dirt is as useless to men as it was before is an irony both heathen and Christian.

SWEDES

Heatho-Reams

GEATS

Jutes

Skane

Heorot

DANES

Eider

Gifthas

Heathobards

Wylfings(?)

Vandals

Vistula

FRISIANS

Hetware

FRANKS

Meuse

Rhine

Elbe

The Geography of *Beowulf*

FAMILY TREES

I. THE ROYAL HOUSE OF THE GEATS

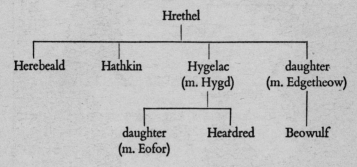

Hrethel

Herebeald · Hathkin · Hygelac (m. Hygd) · daughter (m. Edgetheow)

daughter (m. Eofor) · Heatdred · Beowulf

2. THE ROYAL HOUSE OF THE DANES (SCYLDINGS)

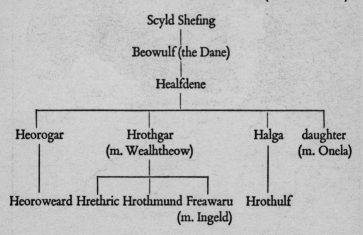

Scyld Shefing

Beowulf (the Dane)

Healfdene

Heorogar · Hrothgar (m. Wealhtheow) · Halga · daughter (m. Onela)

Heoroweard · Hrethric · Hrothmund · Freawaru (m. Ingeld) · Hrothulf

3. THE ROYAL HOUSE OF THE SWEDES (SCYLFINGS)

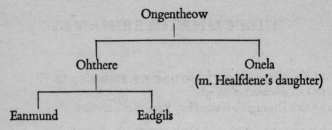

INDEX OF PROPER NAMES

ABEL Killed by Cain, his brother. Genesis iv, 8.

ALFHERE Kinsman of Wiglaf.

ASHHERE Hrothgar's counsellor, Yrmenlaf's brother.

BATTLE-REAMS Tribe of Norway, living in modern Romerike, north of Oslo.

BEANSTAN Breca's father.

BEOW or BEOWULF Danish king, son of Scyld, father of Healfdene.

BEOWULF Son of Edgetheow the Waymunding; nephew of Hygelac.

BRECA Son of Beanstan; chief of the Brondings.

BRISINGS See 1195n.

BRONDINGS Unidentified tribe.

CAIN Killer of Abel, his younger brother; first fratricide; father of all monsters.

DANES Hrothgar's people, also called Scyldings.

DAYRAVEN Champion of the Franks.

EADGILS Swedish prince, son of Ohthere, brother of Eanmund. 2354n.

EANMUND Swedish prince, son of Ohthere, younger brother of Eadgils.

EARNA-NESS A headland in Geatland. (*Earn*: eagle.)

EDGELAF Father of Unferth.

EDGETHEOW A Waymunding who married the only daughter of the Geat king Hrethel; slayer of Heatholaf; Beowulf's father.

EDGEWELA A Danish king otherwise unknown.

EOFOR Geat warrior, slayer of Ongentheow; son of Wonred; brother of Wulf; husband of Hygelac's daughter.

EOMER Son of Offa the Angle.

EORMENRIC The famous king of the East Goths.

FINN King of the East Frisians, ruler also of the Jutes; son of Folcwalda; husband of Hildeburgh. 1068n.

FITELA Nephew (and son) of Sigemund.

FOLCWALDA Father of Finn.

FRANKS The Franks, under the Merovingian kings; also called Hugas; the Frisians and Hetware are their tributaries; enemies of the Geats. 2354n.

FREAWARU Hrothgar's daughter; to marry Ingeld.

FRISIANS The Frisians, whether East (Finn's people) or West (tributaries of the Franks).

FRODA King of the Heathobards, father of Ingeld. Killed by the Danes.

GARMUND Father of Offa the Angle.

GEATS Beowulf's people, inhabitants of modern Gotarike in Southern Sweden. Also called Weather-Geats.

GIFTHAS An East Germanic tribe.

GRENDEL Monster killed by Beowulf; descendant of Cain.

GUTHLAF Danish follower of Hnæf, then of Hengest.

HALF-DANES Hnæf's people, tributaries of the Danes. Possibly Jutes.

HALGA Younger brother of Hrothgar; father of Hrothulf.

HAMA Hero who escaped from Eormenric with the Brising necklace.

HARETH Father of Hygd.

HATHKIN Second son of Hrethel, whom he succeeds, having accidentally killed his elder brother Herebeald. Killed by Ongentheow.

HEALFDENE King of the Danes, son of Beowulf the Dane; father of Heorogar, Hrothgar, Halga and (?) Ursula.

HEARDRED Geat king, son of Hygelac and Hygd. Killed by Onela.

HEATHOBARDS Ingeld's people, enemies of the Danes.

HEATHOLAF A Wylfing, killed by Edgetheow.

HELMINGS Wealhtheow's family.

HEMMING Kinsman of Offa and of Eomer.

HENGEST Leader of the Danes (Half-Danes) after Hnæf's death. Probably identical with Hengest the Jute who conquered Kent.

HEOROGAR Danish king, Hrothgar's elder brother.

HEOROT Hrothgar's hall. Its site was probably near modern Lejre,

Roskilde, Zealand. (*Heorot:* hart – a royal beast, to be seen on the sceptre found at Sutton Hoo.)

HEOROWEARD Heorogar's son; he did not succeed him, perhaps because of his youth.

HEREBEALD Hrethel's eldest son; killed by Hathkin.

HEREMOD Danish tyrant. (*Here:* war; *mod:* mind). 901*n.*

HERERIC Heardred's uncle. Possibly Hygd's brother.

HETWARE Frankish tribe.

HILDEBURGH Wife of Finn; daughter of Hoc; sister of Hnæf.

HNÆF Son of Hoc; brother of Hildeburgh; leader of the Half-Danes.

HOC Father of Hnæf and Hildeburgh.

HREFNAWUDU 'Ravenswood', the Swedish forest where Ongentheow killed Hathkin.

HREOSNABEORGH A hill in Geatland.

HRETHEL King of the Geats, Hygelac's father.

HRETHRIC Son of Hrothgar and Wealhtheow; elder brother of Hrothmund. In tradition, killed by Hrothulf.

HRONESNESS Headland in Geatland. (*Hron:* whale.)

HROTHGAR King of the Danes.

HROTHMUND Hrothgar's son, Hrethric's brother.

HROTHULF Son of Halga; Hrothgar's nephew. 1017*n.*

HRUNTING Unferth's sword.

HUGAS The Franks whom Hygelac attacked.

HUNLAF Father of one of Hnæf's followers.

HYGD Hygelac's wife, Hareth's daughter.

HYGELAC King of the Geats, Beowulf's uncle. Fell in a raid on the Frisians and the Franks in the year 521.

INGELD Son of Froda; prince of the Heathobards; husband of Freawaru.

INGWINE A name for the Danes.

MEROVINGIAN, THE The King of the Franks.

NAILING The sword Beowulf took from Dayraven.

OFFA King of the Angles in Angeln. Ancestor of Offa I of Mercia.

OHTHERE Son of Ongentheow the Swede; elder brother of Onela; father of Eanmund and Eadgils.

ONELA Ohthere's brother and successor; husband of Ursula.

ONGENTHEOW Swedish king, father of Ohthere and Onela; slayer of Hathkin.

OSLAF Danish follower of Hengest.

RAVENSWOOD See Hrefnawudu.

SCYLD Founder of the Danish royal house, the Scyldings. 1*n*.

SCYLDINGS Descendants of Scyld; the Danish royal family; hence Danes in general.

SCYLFINGS The Swedish royal family; hence Swedes in general.

SHEFING Son of Sheaf.

SIGEMUND Son of Wæls; father and uncle of Fitela; conqueror of the dragon Fafnir. 875*n*.

SWEDES The Swedes of east central Sweden, northern neighbours of the Geats.

SWERTING Hygelac's mother's father.

UNFERTH Son of Edgelaf; Hrothgar's counsellor. 499*n*.

URSULA Healfdene's daughter, Onela's wife.

WÆLS Father of Sigemund.

WAYLAND The smith of the gods, the northern Vulcan.

WAYMUNDINGS The family of Wiglaf, Weoxstan and Beowulf. 2596*n*.

WEALHTHEOW Hrothgar's queen.

WEATHERS, WEATHER-GEATS 'Storm-loving' Geats.

WENDEL Vandal.

WEOXSTAN Wiglaf's father.

WIGLAF Son of Weoxstan; a Waymunding and a kinsman of Beowulf. 2596*n*.

WITHERGYLD A Heathobard warrior, probably father of the young warrior of 2044.

WONRED Father of Eofor and Wulf.

WULF Eofor's brother, son of Wonred.

WULFGAR Prince of the Vandals; Hrothgar's chamberlain.

WYLFINGS A Germanic tribe.

YRMENLAF Ashhere's younger brother.